KU-204-964

LIKE FLIES FROM AFAR

K. FERRARI

Translated from the Spanish by
Adrian Nathan West

BLACKTHORN

This paperback edition published in Great Britain in 2021 by Black Thorn,
an imprint of Canongate Books

First published in Great Britain in 2020
by Canongate Books Ltd, 14 High Street, Edinburgh EH1 1TE

blackthornbooks.com

First published in 2018 by Penguin Random House Grupo Editorial, S.A.

1

Copyright © K. Ferrari, 2018
Translation copyright © Adrian Nathan West, 2020

The right of K. Ferrari to be identified as the
author of this work has been asserted by him in accordance
with the Copyright, Designs and Patents Act 1988

British Library Cataloguing-in-Publication Data
A catalogue record for this book is available on
request from the British Library

ISBN 978 1 78689 699 5

Designed by Richard Oriolo

Printed and bound in Great Britain by Clays Ltd, Elcograf S.p.A.

MIX
Paper from
responsible sources
FSC
www.fsc.org
FSC® C018072

K. Ferrari was born in Buenos Aires. He is the author of several novels, collections of short fiction and a book of non-fiction. He is the winner of the Casa de las Américas Prize. *Like Flies from Afar* is the first of his books to be translated into English and is published in Argentina, Spain, Italy, France and the US.

Adrian Nathan West is the author of *The Aesthetics of Degradation*. He is a contributor to the *Times Literary Supplement* and the *Literary Review*; his essays, short fiction and translations have also appeared in the *New York Review of Books*, *McSweeney's*, the *London Review of Books* and other publications.

@a_nathanwest | anathanwest.com

To

Leo Oyola

and

Carlos Salem,

for their unexpected camaraderie

In memory of

Jonathan "Kiki" Lezcano,

young and poor,

murdered by the police

Maybe I'm not sure what I mean. I guess mostly what I mean is that there can't be no personal hell because there ain't no personal sins.

—JIM THOMPSON

War konsequent nur in seiner Gier nach Reichtum und in seinem Haß gegen die Leute, die ihn hervorbringen.

—KARL MARX

If there was a market, he would have sold his chances for one thin dime.

—DAVID GOODIS

If someone wants to read this book as a regular old thriller, that's their choice.

—RODOLFO WALSH

CONTENTS

Disclaimer: What you are about to read is a work of fiction.

Any resemblance to real persons, living or dead, or to incidents blah blah fucking blah.

PART I

BELONGING

TO THE

EMPEROR

1 MR. MACHI LEANS BACK into his armchair, sinks his hand into the blond mane moving rhythmically between his legs, and shuts his eyes. The first rays of morning sun filter through the window in a triangle, making the fountain pen shimmer as they descend over the desk, with its two half-empty glasses, the miniature of Norberto Fontana's Dodge, the antique telephone, the open bindle, the mound of coke, the credit card with its edges frosted from use, and the dirty ashtray, before coming to rest on a framed family photo of Mr. Machi, ten years younger, smiling next to his two children and his wife on a Mediterranean beach. When the vertex of the luminous triangle touches the blond mane, its movements become less rhythmic, following along with the spasms shaking the body of Mr. Machi, who grabs a fistful of blond hair as an orgasm roars out of him with muffled snorts. Then he collapses into the armchair, loosens the knot in his necktie, takes a gold Dupont lighter from the top drawer of the desk, and lights a Montecristo while the woman fixes her hair, wipes the corners of her lips, and sucks down a line.

"You want?" she asks.

She's got a young face, hardly marked by age, and the mascara dripping from her left eye gives her a certain air of negligence, abandon, desperation.

Mr. Machi thinks of his heart problems and the little blue pill he took less than an hour ago, which guarantees his still-relentless organ a slow, even cavalier diminution.

"No, no," he answers, with tobacco smoke in his mouth, then exhales, letting it mingle with that growing triangle of light shining through the window, drawing—the light and the smoke—figures in the air that no one else will bother looking at.

The young woman with the blond hair sniffs—once, twice, three times—and curses, smug and sassy, at the coke, her fate, the triangle of light foretelling another beautiful day—damn it—and the taste of Mr. Machi's sperm in her mouth.

"I'm going, Luis," she announces.

"Shut the door, I've got to stay a while longer. Tell Eduardo and Pereyra to make sure everyone shows up early tonight, okay? Remember, the Mexicans are coming . . ."

"Relax, I've got them under control. We'll see each other tonight, babe," the young woman says, taking leave of Mr. Machi with a kiss on the neck. He lets her kiss him and goes on amusing himself with the smoke from his Montecristo, as though she no longer existed—as though, his desires sated, the girl with the blond hair and the golden nose were nothing more than an irritation. Then, when she turns and heads for the door, hips shifting in her skirt, he takes a look at her ass.

Tomorrow I'm going to crack that wide open, he thinks.

Now alone in his office, he goes to the bathroom and looks at himself in the mirror.

In the mirror, Mr. Machi sees success.

And what is success for Mr. Machi?

He smiles and thinks: Success is me.

Success is a blond bimbo sucking your cock, Luisito, he thinks, smiling into the mirror—success is the taste of a Montecristo. Success is that little blue pill and ten mil in the bank.

He relights the cigar waiting for him in the ashtray on his desk and dials a number on the antique phone. The triangle of light has now taken over the office, leaving no doubt that morning is here.

"Hello," the woman's voice responds, sluggish and bewildered, laying extra stress on the *lo*.

"Hey, I just finished up, I'll be heading back in a bit."

"You just finished up?" the harridan asks. "How nice of you to call. Did you at least wash up first?"

"Mirta, please, don't break my balls. Get something going for breakfast, I'll be home in an hour, give or take," Mr. Machi says, more bored than angry.

"Fine, I'll tell Gladis to make something, if you like." The malice in her words seems to make her feisty. "Ah, no, I'll have to tell Herminia . . ."

"Again with this, Mirta," Mr. Machi says. He takes

5

another drag from his Montecristo and wonders why, since he's still feeling the effects of the little pill, he didn't just tell the girl with the blond hair and the green skirt to stick around so he could give it to her in the ass.

"To what do I owe the honor of your presence at breakfast, if I may be so bold as to ask?" With each word, his wife's voice, Mirta's voice, emerges further from its stupor, her mounting rage evident in her S's, like the hissing of a serpent.

"It's my house, isn't it?" says Mr. Machi, running out of patience. "You're my wife, yeah? So hop to it, whip me up something decent for breakfast . . . I'll be there in an hour, give or take."

He hangs up.

Ball-breaker, he thinks.

He decides, despite the little blue pill and his heart problems, he'll do another rail before he goes.

2 "GOOD MORNING, SIR, everything in order?" says the gorilla with the shaved head—eyes attentive, arms crossed behind his back, no expression on his vacant face—who watches over the garage door in the basement of El Imperio.

"What's up," Mr. Machi responds with a clenched jaw. He snaps his fingers and stretches out his hand.

"Keys," he says.

"Keys," he repeats, not giving time to react.

The gorilla with the shaved head moves quickly, with an agility startling for his big, heavy body.

"Sir," he says with no look on his face, dropping the BMW keys into the outstretched hand of Mr. Machi, who goes on walking without even thinking of the word *thanks*.

"Wait for me to leave, then wait a little longer, and after that, you can get some shut-eye, fat-ass," Mr. Machi says, looking elsewhere and still not slowing his step.

The BMW beeps twice. He gets in. The feel of the seat is luxurious. He chose the leather himself.

It's like stroking a young girl's ass, Mr. Machi thinks.

He pulls off his tie, stuffs it in his suit pocket, and tilts the rearview mirror to look at himself. He makes a face. It would have been a smile if not for the coke. He inspects his eyes, his teeth, his gums, and finally his nostrils, looking for residue. There isn't any. He readjusts the mirror and thinks once more about success.

This car is success, Luisito, that grade-A coke, buddy, your collection of Italian silk ties, just think, even that ball-breaker Mirta is success.

He looks for his Versace sunglasses in the glove compartment and puts them on. Now, now he's ready. He twists the key in the ignition and the BMW motor turns over, mute and powerful. No sooner have the garage doors closed behind the taillights of the black car turning the wrong way down Balcarce to Belgrano than the gorilla with the shaved head spits on the floor, loosens his tie, and shakes his head, uttering a verdict: "Cocksucking son of a bitch."

3 A BLACK BOLT OF LIGHTNING shoots across General Paz at seven in the morning, leaving looks of astonishment and envy in its wake. Mr. Machi feels them like a caress, those looks of envy at his fortune striking the body of the BMW that seems to glide over the asphalt until it reaches the Acceso Norte headed toward the Panamericana Highway. His cell phone starts ringing while the turnoff opens up, then disappears behind him as the black bolt of lightning veers onto the Panamericana.

"Machi," he answers.

"Hey, Pa, sorry to bother you right now but I need to know if this fucking book fell out of my backpack in your car the other day, I need it for class, and . . ."

Mr. Machi, who's already stopped listening, drops the phone in the passenger seat to turn on his hands-free and looks around for his daughter's book. When he puts in the earpiece, she's still explaining how urgent it is that he find it.

". . . I've got a midterm this week and it turns out . . ."

A snatch of something orange and angular peeks over the passenger seat next to the door. Mr. Machi, without slowing down or taking his left hand off the wheel, lunges over and grabs it. It's the book: *The Order of Things*.

"It's here, Luciana," Mr. Machi says, interrupting his daughter's monologue. "Come by the house and grab it when you feel like it. Or by El Imperio. I'm gonna hang up now, I'm driving, babe."

"Okay, Pa, I'll come by tonight with Fe then. We'll see you at like nine. Love you," the girl says, but Mr. Machi doesn't hear her. He hangs up after the word *babe* to give his full concentration to the pleasure of piloting the black bolt of lightning gliding over the asphalt of the Panamericana.

He doesn't want to think about his kids, not about Luciana and especially not about Alan. And he doesn't need to wonder what success is, because he can feel it in the potent purr of the accelerator beneath his right foot, in the cushioned upholstery, in the power steering, in the sunlight and the stares of astonishment and envy reflecting off the BMW's gloss finish.

Less than half a mile past the second tollbooth, Mr. Machi feels the wheel jerk and the car, which was gliding over the pavement like a black bolt of lightning, lurches left.

I popped a tire, he thinks.

Right front, he thinks.

He straightens the BMW with almost professional finesse and pulls it onto the shoulder.

"Shit," Mr. Machi exclaims.

Shit.

Shit.

It must be twenty, twenty-five years since I've blown a tire, he thinks. This is what I get for dropping two hundred Gs on a car?

Then, without cutting the engine, he leans his head on the upholstery he selected himself and shuts his eyes for a second. He needs to muster his patience and fortitude before getting out of the car. Above all, he must be ready to put up with the looks of scorn born of resentment on the faces of the passersby in their ramshackle Dunas, Peugeot 504s, and Renault 19s—cars that cost what he spends on a whore or on a lunch out—as they pass the BMW stranded on the roadside, the same BMW they saw shoot past minutes before like a black bolt of lightning. He knows all those poor bastards will be over the moon to see him stranded there with a blown tire.

A tiny victory for their minuscule lives, he thinks.

And so, as the first batch of Dunas, Peugeot 504s, and Renault 19s passes, before getting out to make sure he's got a flat, he opens his daughter's book and reads:

"This book first arose out of a passage in Borges, out of the laughter that shattered, as I read the passage, all the familiar landmarks of my thought."

What?

He shakes his head. He reads a little more and figures out what he's reading is a ludicrous inventory, a stupid list a five-year-old kid could have made up.

This is what I pay tuition for? he thinks. So she can read this horseshit? It'd be one thing if she studied law or engineering, but no . . .

So this is who Luciana reveres? Guys like this dickhead who gets off on a list a five-year-old kid could have made up, these are the people his daughter reads with devotion in a department that hits him up for $450 every month? These are her philosophers, her sociologists, her thinkers? This is the culture she gets from those professors while he foots the bill for their salaries? What the fuck are they good for, anyway? Could they have built up an empire from nothing, the way he did? And if their kids get the notion to go off to college, could they cough up $450 a month? Eh? Could they?

His hand tenses around the book.

"This book first arose out of a passage in Borges," he reads again.

Borges wrote that? So that makes him Argentina's greatest writer? Mr. Machi congratulates himself for never bothering to read him. Then he reads on, just to piss himself off more.

"But what is it impossible to think, and what kind of impossibility are we faced with here?" he reads.

Mr. Machi opens the window in indignation and throws the book with the orange cover into the middle of the Panamericana. Euphoric, he watches how one, two, three cars pass by before he steps out of the BMW with the word *losers* trembling in his mouth.

4

"ROADSIDE ASSISTANCE will be there in an hour at the latest, sir, thank you for calling," a gentle but impersonal voice tells him over the phone.

"An hour?" Mr. Machi roars. "Are you fucking kidding me? You know how much my premium is? If I gotta wait an hour, I'll cancel my policy and change the damn tire myself. What's your name?"

"My name's Fernando, sir. The mechanic has—"

"First and last name, pal, and your personnel number," Mr. Machi interrupts. "I'm gonna have a little chat with López Lecube when I cancel," he adds in a threatening tone. It's evident from his voice that he's an old hand at both: interrupting and threatening.

"Sir, please understand . . ." pleads the distant and gentle Fernando.

"Come on, pal, I don't have all day. Your full name, spit it out . . ."

"Please hold for a second, sir," and Mr. Machi is treated to ten seconds of a Muzak version of "Für Elise."

Now Fernando is thanking him for remaining on the line. They've managed to clear up a few difficulties and help will be there in twenty minutes or less. "Thank you for calling the Carbajales Insurance Company."

"All right, kid. Twenty minutes." This is Mr. Machi's final warning to Fernando.

Then he walks around to the blown tire to see what's what. Poking out from the deflated rubber are three caltrops. He pulls one out and looks it over.

I haven't seen one of these fuckers since the workers from the textile mill had their big strike, he thinks.

What year was that? '74, '75? Isabel's administration, anyway.

Those commie shitheads used to throw caltrops in the road so we couldn't get away, he remembers. And the memory puts him on alert. The great beast of paranoia stirs inside Mr. Machi and starts to sniff around: if there are caltrops in my tire, it's because somebody threw them at me. And Mr. Machi knows he's an easy target with his two-hundred-thousand-dollar car.

In his glove box is a Glock .45, a gift from his friend Loco Wilkinson. Mr. Machi takes it out, makes sure there's one in the chamber and the safety's off. And now, with the Glock pointed at the ground and the great beast of paranoia fully awake and alert inside him, he walks to the trunk to get out the spare.

And this is where the story really begins.

STUFFED

PART II

STUFFED

5 THE SAME BEAST that put Mr. Machi on guard prevents him at first from seeing what's right in front of him.

He doesn't look at the lock when he opens the trunk. He doesn't even look for the spare. He just reaches in, feels around blindly, the Glock pointed at the ground, eyes scanning his perimeter: first both sides, then behind, making sure no one's creeping up on him. He feels it before he sees it, something sticky and damp on his hand as it stretches toward the spare. He pulls back quickly, as if he's been bitten by a spider.

His hand—sticky and damp—is also red. Now his eyes turn toward the trunk. Now he sees.

He slams the trunk, drops the Glock, and bends over heaving, but he doesn't puke. Mr. Machi coughs and looks down at the Glock as if it's the first time he's ever laid eyes on it.

What's the point of owning a piece like that if, as he now knows, he's incapable of firing it?

Mr. Machi reacquaints himself with the fact that for

men of his sort, murder, like so much else, is something you buy preassembled. So he wipes his sticky, damp hand on his suit pants, stands up straight, heads back to the driver's side door, and puts the Glock back in the glove box, his heart still pounding out of his chest. He sits there for a while in the BMW's bucket seat, which for some reason no longer feels so soft.

No way, he thinks. But there's no doubting the dark red on his hand and the thing he saw in the trunk.

He's got to do something. He's stunned, muddled. Come on, Luisito, get a grip.

He opens his wallet and takes out his license. He cuts out two thick lines on the dash and snorts them up greedily. The cold rush of the coke rouses him.

First confirm. Then decide. He goes back to the trunk and opens it.

It's as though the BMW were pregnant with a man in a blue suit covered in blood. In the fetal position, seeming to embrace himself, the dead man nearly fills Mr. Machi's trunk.

The cocaine has him thinking quick and clear. Mr. Machi realizes the first order of business is calling back the insurance company.

"Carbajales Insurance Company, good morning, my name is Patricia, how can I assist you?" Another gentle, impersonal voice, this time female.

"Gimme Fernando," Mr. Machi tells her, trying to steady the trembling in his voice.

"Please stay on the line for a moment while I transfer you over, sir," the impersonal voice says before giving way to "Für Elise." Twenty seconds pass, endless for Mr. Machi, before Fernando comes on, begs his pardon for the delay, and asks how he can be of assistance.

"I don't want the mechanic," Mr. Machi shouts. "Listen closely, pal, do *not* send the mechanic that I called for, okay?"

"My apologies, sir. Could you please let me know your license plate number?"

"VTN-431," Mr. Machi says, and repeats that he no longer wants the mechanic they were going to send.

Fernando—who now knows who he's talking to and remembers their earlier conversation and the mention of the name López Lecube—asks if there's been a problem, tells him the mechanic is on his way, that he will be there in fifteen minutes to change Mr. Machi's tire, just as requested.

"Don't send him, pal. Make absolutely sure he doesn't show up here, get it?" Mr. Machi says.

Fernando's voice, less gentle and impersonal now than anxious and confused, replies: No problem, he'll cancel the service order, and thank you for calling . . .

But Mr. Machi's already hung up.

He takes another look at the blue-suited cadaver in his trunk. Suppressing the disgust touching the lifeless body provokes, he turns its head around to see if he knows the guy. But Mr. Machi can't see the man's face. There isn't one. Where a face should be, there's only wreckage: bones, organic matter, blood, and gunpowder. Mr. Machi feels himself heave again and tries to steady his stomach. He wonders: how close did they have to be when they shot him to do that to his face?

He wonders: how long has this guy been dead?

But more than anything, he wonders what a corpse is doing in his two-hundred-thousand-dollar BMW. And how the fuck it got there.

6 NOW HE HAS A PRACTICAL matter to deal with: to ditch the body, he needs to get off the Panamericana, and to do that, he needs to get the spare tire out from underneath, no way around it.

Knowing it won't be the last time he touches that cold, stiff body, doubled over with a bloody mess where there ought to be a face, Mr. Machi pushes the thing with all his might to the very back of the trunk. Then he starts jerking on the tire. His sunglasses fall and one of their hinges chips on the ground.

Son of a bitch, Mr. Machi thinks.

He picks them up and sets them on top of his head like a hairband. He feels the weight of the stares coming from every car that passes by. He sees the smug smiles of the drivers in their Dunas, Peugeot 504s, and Renault 19s, looking at a car they'll never afford stranded on the side of the road—he knows they won't be able to resist sharing this tiny triumph with their wives, and that they'll point at him, asking:

"What could be giving that guy in the black car so much trouble?"

They'll joke, they'll laugh.

"If it's so hard for him to change a tire, why doesn't he call roadside assistance or something?"

"Maybe the car cost so much he can't afford the insurance," the wittiest among them will say.

But these jokes, which would normally have made Mr. Machi's blood boil, now don't disturb him in the least. Or, if they do, it's for a different reason. His worry now is that he's drawing attention to himself—to his backbreaking efforts, to his broken-down BMW—and that every one of those poor fuckers looking at him and smirking is a potential witness.

Finally he manages to pull out the tire, the jack, the lug wrench from beneath the stiff, heavy arm of the corpse.

He changes the tire as fast as he can.

Like he was working the pit for Norberto Fontana, he thinks.

Then he puts the powerful engine in gear and jets off—a two-hundred-thousand-dollar lightning bolt on the asphalt of the Panamericana—leaving behind a mound of incriminating evidence on the roadside: the lug wrench, the jack, and the punctured tire.

7 MR. MACHI BUTTONS his Scappino blazer and flips up the lapels to cover the bloodstains streaking his white Armani shirt. He doesn't look at himself in the rearview. If he did, he'd see he's aged ten years in the past fifteen minutes.

He accelerates, no fixed course in mind, and makes a call.

"You have reached . . ." the voicemail of his security chief begins.

Where's that dope when I need him? Mr. Machi wonders. Since when did he decide he doesn't need to bother taking my calls?

". . . the number of Robledo Pereyra . . ."

Don't I pay him twice what he used to make? Didn't I take him on after that shitshow in Ciudadela? Wasn't it my lawyers who pulled his balls out of the fire? Didn't I spend a fortune on witnesses? But hey, it was no big deal, because that's what I do: Business. Clean business, dirty business. Business.

What I don't do is deal with bodies in trunks, for fuck's

sake, he thinks with mounting irritation. That's what I pay him for, and now he won't pick up.

"You have reached the number of Robledo Pereyra, please leave a message . . ."

Plus, I've got you by the balls, Cesspit—now he's having a full-blown conversation in his head—and we both know it: so what the fuck are you doing not picking up?

"You have reached the number of Robledo Pereyra, please leave a message after the tone."

"Call me, Cesspit. It's urgent," is the message Mr. Machi finally leaves, his voice trembling more from fury than from fear.

A minute passes.

Mr. Machi glances at his white gold Rolex.

Two.

He looks back at the Rolex, taps instinctively with his index finger on the glass. Then he takes the first exit off the Panamericana.

Imagine that moron's had a heart attack and I'm waiting for a dead man to call me back, Mr. Machi thinks. That's how Loco Wilkinson died—a miserable, rotten heart attack in his sleep.

He smiles at the thought of Cesspit Pereyra's giant inert body on a bed with white sheets—his thick, graying mustache over his rigid mouth, his beard climbing halfway up his cheek, a cigarette burning down in the ashtray, his eyes staring into nothingness—while his cell phone rings and rings. But this image immediately reminds Mr. Machi of the shredded face and blue suit in his trunk, and his smile vanishes, transformed into a look of dread. He shakes his head, as though trying to keep the thought of it at bay.

No, no way, who gave him permission to die? he thinks, wavering between perplexity and indignation.

But if he's not dead, then why won't he pick up?

There's a pause in his deliberations. He advances up a tree-lined street and turns onto the first dirt road to look for an empty lot.

What if he's the one who stashed it there? The question comes out of nowhere and smacks Mr. Machi across the face. On the chessboard in his mind, a few scattered pieces shift into place.

What if he's the one who put the dead guy there—he presses on, still incredulous, but horrified by his growing conviction—and that's the reason he won't pick up?

Who else could lug a dead body down to the basement of El Imperio, open the trunk of the BMW without breaking the lock, dump the corpse, and disappear, just like that? Only Cesspit, the direct supervisor of that bald-headed gorilla who guards the garage. A scary guy, Pereyra, Mr. Machi thinks. And complicated. You never know what's what with him: sometimes he's a roughneck, sometimes a gentleman. Always dangerous though. Very dangerous.

That son of a bitch is trying to fuck me so he can rest

easy about the thing with Ciudadela, he thinks. Or the thing with that fuckhead from Entre Ríos. Or the thing with Don Rogelio. Or for cash. Son of a bitch.

Then his cell rings: Pereyra.

Mr. Machi doesn't pick up.

I'm all alone, he thinks.

PART III

TAMED

8 BACK WHEN MR. MACHI met Robledo Pereyra, no one called him Cesspit. Even now, no one calls him that except for Mr. Machi. People who know him from the wild years of the dictatorship call him "the Fox"; people who know him from his boxing days call him "Knuckles"; his family calls him by his childhood nickname, Robi, which he can't stand; his closest friends call him Pereyra. Mr. Machi dubbed him Cesspit the first day they met, and it was his personal privilege to do so.

Alejandro Wilkinson introduced them a long time back.

"You need a guy like this, Machi," Wilkinson told him when the two men showed up one day, "and he needs you to help him out of a little predicament. A good lawyer, a decent alibi, you catch my drift, people know me too well for me to be of much help, but you, you're clean. And if you do this for him, he'll have your back from here on out. This guy's a rock . . . Tell him, Pereyra."

A real bag of shit, this Pereyra. One foulmouthed motherfucker.

He never says "Zip it," he says "Shut your cock-holster," or "How's about I sew your fucking face shut." He never says "That dude over there," he says "That pencil-dicked gimp." He never says "Check out that hot number," he says "Get a load of that piece of skirt with the dick-sucking lips over there."

And that first time was no exception.

Explaining himself, he never told Mr. Machi "I've got a bit of a problem," he said, "I'm in it up to my fucking balls." He didn't talk about murder preceded by torture, he said, "Damn right I wasted that Jew fuck, I even made him shit his pants before he kicked the bucket." He didn't say it was a matter of vengeance, something he'd been waiting years for; he said, "I've been dreaming of taking that shithead out since I had two hairs on my dick." He didn't say the deceased happened to have a relative employed in the justice department, and that this was why there was an investigation already closing in on him; he said, "And apparently that kike was kin to some swinging dick downtown who's trying to nail me to the fucking wall." He didn't finish up by complaining that his boss had left him out in the cold; instead he spat and said, "After all the shit I been through, scumbag ditches me like I'm Joe Jerkoff and tells me I gotta fix shit on my own."

"Don't rile yourself up. I'll talk to one of my lawyers and we'll get you three or four witnesses to place you somewhere else. Then you can come work for me. What'd you say you make?" Mr. Machi said after listening to the man's explanations.

Pereyra gave him a number, followed by the phrase: "That's what that greedy rat fuck pays me."

"You're a Cesspit, Pereyra," Mr. Machi said, cracking up at the comparison, and added, "You're gonna need to work on your vocabulary, eh? You work for me now, Cesspit. I'll pay you double, how's that sound?" and the sobriquet and the doubled salary served as confirmation of ownership. Mr. Machi had bought himself some muscle same as a guy goes to a pet shop to buy himself a dog.

"Start getting my security together, then tell me whatever you need," Mr. Machi said with a handshake. It was the first and last time they bothered pretending to be equals.

"Leave us alone now, Cesspit, I want to talk with our friend Wilkinson here," Mr. Machi said.

"Of course, Mr. Machi," Pereyra responded, already knowing his place.

9 "TAKE THAT DIPSHIT over there in the yellow tank top," Pereyra said, "you think he even knows who the commie fuck he's got stamped on there is?"

Wilkinson enjoyed Pereyra's fits of indignation. And they call me loco, he thought.

"Because at least you all knew—maybe we scared you shitless, but you knew. These stupid fucks though . . ."

"So what are you gonna do, you gonna tell him?" Wilkinson egged him on for his own amusement.

They were at a roadhouse alongside Route 12 headed toward Misiones, eating sweetbreads and drinking red wine. Alejandro Wilkinson, who boasted of never drinking wines that cost less than two hundred dollars, thought, Here goes my last stab at populism, and chuckled. They were on their way to pick up matching 4x4s from Brazil and a package of coke Romero had sent.

"Reckon I will," Pereyra said. Then he wiped off his mouth with the back of his hand and turned to the neighboring table: "Hey you, dickhead, get over here . . ."

"Me?" the kid in the yellow tank top asked, perplexed.

With that freckled face and those frightened eyes, he couldn't have been a day over twenty. On his yellow tank top, under the face of Che Guevara, was the legend BETTER TO DIE ON YOUR FEET THAN TO LIVE ON YOUR KNEES.

"Yeah, you, motherfucker," Pereyra said.

The kid in the yellow tank top was sitting with two of his friends. They were drinking beers and talking about some girls they had met in the last town over. They were traveling in a dinged-up Gol, and their backpacks were on the ground. Wilkinson smiled, shook his head, and chewed. He thought about the exquisite taste of the sweetbreads and the pleasures of going on the road with Pereyra, who had just pulled out a .45, aimed it between Che Guevara's eyes, and repeated the words: "I said, get over here."

Frightened, the kid blubbered the word *please* while his friends beat a retreat, knocking over a beer bottle that fell to the floor and broke, and the owner of the roadhouse pleaded for calm.

"You shut your beak, this ain't about you," Pereyra ordered.

Then, to the kid in the yellow tank top:

"Stop there."

In the brief silence, nothing could be heard but the clanking of Alejandro Wilkinson's flatware.

"You know who that motherfucker is that you got on your shirt?" Pereyra asked.

"Please, mister . . ."

"Don't 'please, mister' me, fuckhead, do you know or not?"

"No, no. I mean, yeah. Yeah, I know: it's Che, but . . ."

"You read what it says there on that piece of shit muscle shirt you got on?"

"It . . . yeah . . . uh . . ."

"Cool, motherfucker. Then I'll give you ten seconds to choose: live on your knees or die on your feet. Ten, nine, eight . . ."

"But, mister . . ."

"Seven, six . . ."

The kid in the yellow tank top's blubbering turned to sobs as Wilkinson, entertained, wolfed down the last bit of sweetbreads and walked to the cash register to pay.

"Five, four . . ."

"C-come on . . . please . . ."

"Three, two . . ."

"No, please," he got out before kneeling down.

"See, what'd I tell you, Alejandro, look . . . These pussies ain't got a fucking clue. And what about your gay-ass friends? Where'd they run off to? Huh?"

Wilkinson nodded. He put down the money for the sweetbreads, the wine, the beers that the kid in the yellow tank top and his friends hadn't paid for, and laid a crisp hundred on the counter for a tip.

"For your service, and your discretion," he explained.

"Of course, sir," the proprietor said, stuffing the cash into the pocket of a filthy, badly tied apron, "at your service."

"Enough, faggot," Pereyra said, pressing his toe into the kid in the Che tank top, who was still kneeling on the ground sobbing. "Stop, you already picked . . ."

The kid went on sniffling awhile, then stood up slowly, a tremor traveling through his entire body. When he was up, still crying, and tried to utter the word *mister* again, Pereyra stopped him.

"You chose to live, faggot," he said, then shot him once in each knee.

The shots even gave Alejandro Wilkinson a jolt; he hadn't seen them coming. Anxious, he thought: I've created a monster. The last thing this animal needed was a guy like Machi to have his back. Who'll stop him now? But he didn't let his worry show.

"You're off the rails, Pereyra," he said, splitting his sides. "Let's go or we won't make it to Misiones."

"Yeah, let's go," Pereyra said, shrouded in smoke from a freshly lit cigarette.

"You hear that fucker squeal?" he said when they were getting into the car.

A few steps away, on the ground, beneath the kid in the yellow tank top, who was screaming like a madman, a puddle of blood grew and grew.

And grew.

10

"WHAT DO YOU WANT HERE?" Don Rogelio said. He had a place, Doctor Tango, along the same lines as El Imperio, and there had been some—how to put it—disagreement between the two concerning clientele.

"Don Rogelio's old-school, he won't listen, he doesn't get it, he doesn't want to hear it," Mr. Machi had complained a few hours before, like a whiny teenager. "He's not the type you can talk to."

"If he's not someone you can talk to, then that's my line, sir," Cesspit Pereyra said.

"I don't know, the old man's an institution," Mr. Machi said hesitantly, "and he's got some heavyweights of his own, you know . . ."

There was scorn and perplexity in the smile that spread beneath Pereyra's tufted mustache. Heavyweights? he thought. Who does this dumb fuck think he's talking to?

But what he said was: "I think I can handle this, sir."

"Look, Cesspit, keep it clean, I don't want any trouble. I'm looking for an arrangement, something where the both of us can get our slice," Mr. Machi added.

How about you suck on a slice of my dick? Pereyra thought. You want to shake the old bastard down but you don't want no one to get shit on their hands?

But instead, he repeated the words: "Keep it clean, yes, sir, I'm just going to talk to him, let him know what our terms are, nothing else."

"And his boys? You need to take someone from the crew along with you?" Mr. Machi asked, tacitly accepting Pereyra's offer to intervene.

Yeah, shithead, like I don't know what I'm doing, Cesspit thought. Who the fuck do you think you're dealing with? Besides, why do I need to take an army if I'm supposed to go there to play nice like a fucking bitch?

But what he said was: "No, sir, I can handle it on my own. Tonight, if that works for you."

"Okay, but take it easy, Cesspit, no rough stuff, eh?" Mr. Machi warned him one last time, and lamented: it would be so much easier to just negotiate with his children . . .

Say what you mean, pussy! You don't even have the balls to give the order? Pereyra thought as he said, "No need to worry, sir, not a single coarse word."

So that night he went to Doctor Tango, and after encouraging the goons working the door to get lost in a less than amicable way, and informing the security guard inside, an old acquaintance, that all he needed was a few minutes with the boss to talk things over, he walked into the office.

The last of the goons, standing next to the old guy,

pulled out a .38 and aimed it at Pereyra, not menacingly, but as though it were second nature.

That was when Don Rogelio asked him, "What do you want here?"

"What do you want here, *sir*," Cesspit corrected him, then turned to the other: "And you, shit-for-brains, put that thing down."

The goon stood there, imperturbable, imagining the line running straight from his .38 to Pereyra's chest, waiting for the order that Don Rogelio didn't give; instead the old man leaned back in his armchair and asked Pereyra again, this time calling him *sir*, what it was he wanted.

"First thing I want is for you to think of how many times someone's pointed a gun at you," Pereyra said. He ran his tongue over his bristly mustache. He relished this kind of situation, even if he was struggling to get through a sentence without his beloved four-letter words.

He continued, "Now I want you to think of how many times you pointed a gun at someone else."

He paused briefly.

"Then I'd like you to try to imagine how many times that douchebag you got next to you has pointed a gun at somebody or had a gun pointed at him. Same goes for whoever had his job before him."

A few more seconds to add it all up.

"Finally," he went on, "I'd like you to think how many times your friends did all that. And then the friends of your friends. And then multiply that by three, Don Rogelio."

Pereyra's voice was calm, but there was agitation in his gaze, signs of latent violence not easily restrained, like a volcano on the verge of erupting. The goon's beating heart was making his .38 shake. All three of them knew it.

"Now, you need to realize that whatever the number is you came up with, it's way lower than the number of guys ten times harder than that douchebag you got next to you that I go through every day before breakfast," Pereyra said.

The goon had to grab the .38 with his left hand to keep it still. Pereyra smiled again, stroked his mustache, the beard that grew halfway up his cheeks, and finished:

"And I ate a big breakfast today, Don Rogelio. So my recommendation is to tell that douchebag to put down his gun, because otherwise someone's going to end up hurt, and it may well be you. As soon as he does, you and I can talk like civilized people."

Don Rogelio smiled back at Pereyra and reached out his left hand to lower the gun, and his goon sighed with relief, though he would never have admitted it.

"Wait for me outside," he said.

"Sir?" said the goon, fearing his job was on the line.

"Outside," Don Rogelio said, and invited Pereyra to sit down.

"You don't mind if I smoke, do you?" Pereyra asked.

Minutes later, with the smoke of his Parisienne still drifting through the office, Pereyra exited Doctor Tango, taking leave of the bodyguards with a nod of his head, while Don Rogelio lay slung over his desk, a marionette with a snapped neck.

Mr. Machi met with Rogelio's children a few weeks later. This time, it was much simpler to reach an agreement.

11

NOW, YES.

I'm going to tell you a story, just in case, despite everything, you still don't recognize me. Maybe it's the beard. But don't worry, it'll come back to you once I get to talking.

It was in '90 or '91, I don't remember anymore. It happened fast, okay, the whole thing couldn't have lasted more than eight, maybe ten hours. They jerked me out of bed real rough, right in my own home, three blocks from here. Three blocks, think about that . . .

But back to the story. I was saying these ratfucks nabbed me in my sleep. There were three of them: two Jew bastards and a piece of ass so fine, you'd drag your dick through hot coals just to finger-fuck her shadow. Anyway, they threw me into this rattletrap, and next thing I know, they got me tied to a chair next to Hyena Roldán and this other dude I never saw in my life.

These pissants wouldn't say a word to us, you believe that? They didn't talk to us, they didn't smack us up, they didn't do nothin'.

I don't know what the fuck they want, I thought.

What kind of faggot-ass little war do these shitheads think they're fighting, I thought.

Because one thing was clear: if Roldán and I were tied to a chair, one next to the other, then the Jews and the slut and the rest of them—there were four other dudes there, remember now?—were a bunch of hateful little bitches who must have thought they were mixed up in some kind of war.

But like I say, they didn't talk to us, they didn't smack us up, no rough stuff, no nothin'.

We're not like them, they must have thought. They thought they were better than us! They thought they were better than me, those cocksuckers!

So that's how it was: they didn't say nothin', we didn't say nothin'. I mean, Roldán and me didn't say nothin', the other jerkoff was over there singin' his ass off like a fuckin' bird. He offered 'em money, whatever the fuck.

"It'll never happen again," the faggot pleaded. "We were just following orders."

The other assholes there didn't say a word.

"I've got a family," he cried.

Then finally Hyena says to him, "Shut it, pal, if you can't hold on to your dignity, at least don't shit on ours." And right there the little bitch starts whimpering, real soft. But he did shut his trap, at least.

A while later, the slut comes in with a box full of tubes

and gadgets and shit. She plugged a couple of them in. They made this drilling sound.

All right, I thought, now comes the rough stuff.

Christ on a rubber cross, I thought, I'm gonna get whacked by a chick.

But that wasn't the deal. Instead, one by one, starting with me, the bitch tattooed our faces. That's right. A tattoo. They also put up posters around the city with some kind of bullshit slogan. They tattooed us though, get it?

Propaganda, they said.

A tip-off, they explained.

Some bullshit about social justice, they said.

These dumb fucks thought we were playing politics, and with that, they thought they had us beat. I gotta say: we used to fuck 'em up bad, those pinkos didn't know which way was up. We caught 'em flat-flooted and stomped 'em a new asshole. And now they didn't know what to do or who to go after.

Anyway, the pussies vamoosed out of there and told the cops where to find us. They rolled in a few hours later and there we were, tied to these raggedy-ass chairs in some dump of a house in Berazategui, and each one of us with a pretty little tattoo square in the middle of his face. Go ahead, laugh your ass off.

I had to cool my heels a few days and wait for that shit to scar over so they could operate on me and get rid of it. Don't get me wrong, it's not like I thought the bitch did a bad job, but you can't exactly go walking around the street with the word *Torturer* stamped on your mug. People are real scum, you know? They gawk at you, they point.

The surgery cost me an arm and a leg, almost two thou American. Lasers and all types of other shit. It hurt, too. Like you wouldn't fuckin' believe. Post-op was like having ground glass shoved down your dick hole. I mean that.

So I promised myself I was gonna put at least one of those rotten little fuckers in the dirt. And I looked and looked for them. No luck. I asked every small-time punk I could think of, guys that printed fake IDs and shit like that. Nothing. The fuckers didn't know word one about politics but they damn sure knew how to cover their ass: there wasn't a trace of them anywhere.

But I'm a believer, you know. You believe in God, dude? Nah, of course you don't . . . Me, though, I'm a believer. God was gonna help me, right? God wasn't gonna let some pinko shitheads, Jews at that, give me the slip forever.

So the years passed. And now, when I'd nearly forgotten the whole thing, look who I've got here. Because you can say what you want, but I recognize you, douchebag. And if I'm wrong, you look enough like that other piece of shit to do the trick just fine.

Torturer, that's what you wrote on my face, right?

Y'all fucked up one thing big-time: you left me alive. That's not how you play politics, you little bitch; that's not how you win a war. That's not how you do anything.

That's why I tied you to the truck and dragged your ass thirty blocks. That's why I kicked the shit out of you. So you'd learn.

You don't care if I smoke, no?

Torturer, look at you . . .

See this knife? Take a good look, get yourself ready, and say goodbye to your guts.

Get ready, 'cause this is gonna hurt.

It's gonna hurt like a bitch, I promise you.

PART IV

SUCKLING

PIGS

12

THE PHONE RINGS twice more and Mr. Machi doesn't pick up. Confused and terrified, he asks himself what kind of sick shit Pereyra's got up his sleeve. If he's calling, it's because he knows Mr. Machi knows. He imagines him stroking his beard, smiling behind his thick mustache and cigarette.

Money. It's got to be money, Mr. Machi thinks, money's the only thing it can be. But then again, with Pereyra, it could just as well be something else. That unnerves him even further: if it was money, the problem would already be solved. *But.*

He turns round and round in that neighborhood on the outskirts, searching for a street that looks deserted enough to dump the body. But there's someone on every corner: a neighbor lady sweeping and whistling a waltz; some kids knocking back the last beer of the night, even though it's well into the morning; a milkman or delivery boy from the bakery; three or four guys patching up a sidewalk; an old man in a T-shirt on a bench listening to the radio. For Mr. Machi, all this normalcy seems ridiculous and insulting: these simple people shock, even offend him with their routine, gentle, even-keeled movements in this humdrum neighborhood of one-story houses on the fringes of Buenos Aires while he, who would fork over big bucks for that kind of peace, he, who should be at home right now—with all the serenity, security, and comfort of his house in the gated community of El Barrio—is living in the middle of a horror movie.

Why are they all calm and not me? Mr. Machi asks himself. Can these lowlifes pay what I pay to keep myself safe and sound? He shakes his head, hands strangling the wheel as though he suddenly detests the car's soft interior, the grace of its power steering, its flawless black paint job. It doesn't surprise him that this kind of thing happens—the corpse, the trunk, the mystery. What surprises Mr. Machi is that it's happening to him.

It's suddenly clear that all eyes are on his BMW, even more so than normal.

Mr. Machi again asks himself why, and has to struggle to suppress his retching when he imagines blood pouring out of his trunk. But the motive behind the stares is more mundane, and for Mr. Machi, less perilous: it's just that, little by little, his right foot's gotten heavier on the gas, and the BMW, already an anomaly in that area, is cruising over the suburban streets at a velocity far from ordinary in those parts.

I've got to get out of here, he thinks. I've already made too much of a scene.

He turns onto an avenue heading west. After thirty blocks, he looks at the speedometer, just to keep an eye on it, to keep an eye on himself.

Cruise control, he thinks.

But something else calls his attention to the dash. The odometer is stuck on zero. Someone's messed with it. The word *someone* reverberates in his brain until it opens a crack and a doubt slips in.

Could it be that it wasn't Pereyra who took the BMW and stuck a corpse in the trunk? Mr. Machi wonders, and the thought shakes him, makes him remember the face veiled with blood, the bones and the traces of gunpowder, the rigid body folded in on itself, the stiff limbs in the blue suit.

No, no way, he thinks, I don't have enemies, I'm a businessman, businessmen have rivals, competitors, employees, associates, but not enemies.

Enemies are guys like Pereyra, he thinks.

He's the only link between me and anything illegal, he thinks.

Besides, he complains to himself, who the fuck could I have pissed off so bad to make them do a thing like this?

When all's said and done, I'm a good guy, he thinks.

But the crack's already there and doubt is threatening to blow his skull wide open.

Pereyra had been with him almost all night at El Imperio. And if he wanted to take Mr. Machi down, he had easier ways of doing it.

Who has access to the car? Mr. Machi asks himself. How many people?

"How many?" Mr. Machi hears himself say aloud. And just those two words, *how many*, bring him face-to-face with the possibility that more than one person is involved.

No, no, no, he thinks, it can't be, it's got to be Pereyra, because . . .

But something distracts him. Less than fifty meters away, two of Buenos Aires's finest, pistols in hand, are standing next to a patrol car and motioning for him to pull over.

And for a moment, he struggles for breath.

13

THEIR GOOD-COP, BAD-COP routine is so grotesque, it seems like a put-on. But Mr. Machi's nerves make him feel like he's dissolving, like he's no longer himself, but someone else, someone he doesn't even know.

The one playing good cop looks a little thinner. But he's not.

"A person like you," he says, "has got no reason to be in this part of town."

"Could be dangerous," he says.

"We're here to look out for you," he says.

The other—shorter, fat, mustachioed—is the archetypical Buenos Aires flatfoot. He doesn't move the pistol from his hip or his finger from the trigger.

"What you doing around here?" he asks. "You lost or something?"

"Or you out trying to find something?" he asks.

"You got your license and registration?" he asks.

Mr. Machi perspires through the Armani shirt stained with blood beneath his blazer and digs around for his billfold.

"I felt better when I saw you guys," he says, "I don't know this area.

"I was looking to buy a pig," he says.

"I got lost," he says. "Here are my license and registration," he says.

Mr. Machi's pulse is going like a blender. He gives the bad cop the billfold with his license, his registration, the papers for the Glock, and his concealed carry permit. Also the card of a judge he's friendly with and another from the minister of the interior.

Please assist the bearer of this card, Señor Luis Machi, with all means at your disposal, the card reads. But the bad cop doesn't look at it. Instead, he's eyeing up the papers for the Glock.

"Lookee here," he says to his partner, "he's got a gun, too."

And to Mr. Machi: "Can we see it?"

"Of course," Mr. Machi says, cowed. Cowed and uncomfortable in a humiliating role he's far from accustomed to playing. He asks himself when they'll get around to the part about the bribe; his fear keeps him from making the first move. How much could that fat fuck possibly make? Mr. Machi wonders. Cash, that'll solve everything.

"Well, a person like yourself has to take certain precautions, there are a lot of delinquents on the loose," the good cop remarks with a smile straight from a toothpaste ad.

"Exit the vehicle," the bad cop orders. If his face was in an ad, it would be for antacids. Before and after. The bad cop would be before.

"I don't think that's necessary, Sánchez," the good cop says, but the bad one keeps pressing it, even when Mr. Machi is already halfway out of the car:

"Exit the vehicle, please, and let me see your weapon."

They look at the Glock, weigh it in their hands, admire its workmanship.

"Nice piece," the good one sighs. "Congratulations."

"Not like this garbage we're packing," Sánchez says, letting the bad-cop role drop a bit while he palms the holster hanging from his belt, smiles for the first time, and winks. "Just think, we're law enforcement professionals, and we'll never get our hands on one of these, will we, Sosa?"

"True," the good cop, aka Sosa, concedes. "Would you believe, sir, we have to pay for our practice rounds out of our own pocket?"

Mr. Machi doesn't listen to them, he replies on autopilot, lets his years of miscellaneous bribes and kickbacks speak for him while he thinks: I'm calling too much attention to myself here. These two are witnesses, that's a big risk, I gotta clear out and dump this body somewhere else.

"That's a damn shame," he says.

Mr. Machi's autopilot says it's a damn shame—that

he'd like to do what he can to help out with that regrettable situation, what do people expect if not even the forces of order can make a fair day's pay—but then Sánchez cuts him off and brings him back to reality.

"You're missing a bullet here," he says. "It's been fired recently." He's arching his eyebrows, letting the bad cop peep back through.

"The gentleman has a license," Sosa butts in, a good cop through and through. "He doesn't have to explain anything."

"A couple of dogs," Mr. Machi claims, not especially sure why.

"I just scared 'em off," he says.

"I don't know where exactly, over there, I think, on the other side of the highway," he ventures.

Sosa smiles.

Sánchez smiles.

Mr. Machi realizes that it's time. He stops trembling, recovers his composure, and smiles in turn.

"Well now, officers," he says.

And this is why, when he finally puts the BMW in gear—though his wallet is notably lighter, missing several hundred-peso bills, and his Glock is now tucked into Officer Sánchez's belt next to his subpar regulation pistol—Mr. Machi feels like himself again. The two officers wave him off with copious apologies and offers of assistance with whatever he might need, but Mr. Machi, once more master of himself and a master to others, no longer hears them, and pulls off at top speed.

"I need to get this over with now," he says, looking himself in the eyes in his rearview mirror.

But it's not going to be that easy.

14

NOT EVEN TEN MINUTES have passed when he finds the perfect spot: isolated, no gawkers in sight, a barren plot of overgrown grass no one saw him drive to. All that's left is to beat back his nausea and pull it out of the trunk. It.

It, Mr. Machi thinks. He doesn't even let his brain circuits trace out the word *corpse*.

It.

Later, there will be time to figure out who is responsible, he thinks, but first, get rid of it and go home to get some rest.

But he's got to open the trunk, drag it out, throw it in the grass. *It*, which, even if he won't call it by its name, is a blood-drenched cadaver with its face ripped apart by a bullet.

A bullet, Mr. Machi thinks.

"You're missing a bullet here," he hears Sánchez say again. And again, he's rigid with terror.

Impossible, he thinks.

Sánchez's voice reverberates, clear as gin: "It's been fired recently."

Impossible, Mr. Machi thinks, no way they did it with my gun.

But why not? The questions bore through Mr. Machi's lumbering arguments and tangle up into a giant ball that threatens to crush him. They took the car, didn't they? Wasn't the Glock always in the glove box?

Now the Glock is tucked into the belt of a police officer, he remembers. Maybe that's a good thing.

When the dead guy shows up, how's that pig gonna prove he's not the one who iced him?

The idea amuses Mr. Machi.

Enough.

It's time to stop thinking and put his shoulder to the wheel.

He opens his wallet and sucks up the last bit of what's left in the bindle. The coke gives him the coolness he was missing, the courage he's never had, and clears away something of his constantly growing weariness.

The place is promising. The hour, too, Mr. Machi thinks.

Now, he commands himself, and steps out of the BMW. Coasting on that same momentum, he opens the trunk, passes one arm under the body, and grabs the lapel of its blue suit jacket, trying not to look. After two tugs, the body is halfway out. He feels blood on his hands, tears in his eyes, and cold sweat on his forehead. A long-suppressed heave forces its way up his chest, but he manages to get it under control.

"Just a little more, Luisito," he says, encouraging himself. And he gives it another pull.

The body won't give.

Again.

Nothing.

What the fuck is it now? Mr. Machi wonders, pissed.

Must have got caught on something, he thinks.

He knows he has to look, that to dislodge whatever it is he'll have to look at that faceless body in the blue suit, and then, no matter how stubbornly he persists in calling it *it*, it will be transformed into a man.

A dead man.

A dead man with a shredded face.

A dead man with a shredded face drenched in blood.

A dead man with a shredded face drenched in blood in the trunk of his car.

Mr. Machi quashes his vertigo and looks to see what it is that's snagged in the trunk. And this time, his heaving overcomes all resistance and Mr. Machi collapses in the grass, vomits, vomits, and vomits.

When he manages to pull himself up off the ground, he brushes off his Scappino suit, now blotched with blood, puke, and earth.

What next? he asks himself.

Enough, he says to himself, enough.

The cadaver's right hand is shackled to the BMW. Mr. Machi recognizes the object choking off the dead man's wrist. An innocent toy, a fantasy plaything, a secret little trinket.

Secret, he thinks. This changes everything. It means, for example, that Pereyra couldn't have done it alone, because he didn't know. There had to be someone else in the mix. An ally. Maybe a girl.

This changes everything, he repeats to himself.

The questions explode in his chest behind his blood-soaked shirt and vomit-flecked suit. Mr. Machi pushes the body back inside the trunk. And closes the lid.

Secret, he thinks.

The possibilities open up like a fan, and the air they stir up is putrid.

SIRENS

PART V

SIRENS

15

THAT'S HOW IT IS, sooner or later he drops you on your ass. He likes to change it up constantly, doesn't matter what you offer him or how much you put up with, sooner or later it's: adios, you're done.

But hey, it was good while it lasted, right? Or something. Live by the sword, die by the sword. Or maybe dead men tell no tales, I don't know, just pick the cliché that works.

I mean, when I decided I wasn't gonna go on being the girl he just slipped it to now and again in his office or in the changing rooms at El Imperio, that I was gonna be The Lover, I knew I'd have to push Colorada aside, and when I did it, and I didn't look back, then, well, I don't know . . .

My problem is coke. I started snorting it up by the ton, the good shit, with Machi, and now I got a taste for it, big-time.

Anyway, things were tough with Colorada, she's not like the rest of us—firm legs, tight ass, but flat as a board—no, she's got a rack like two melons and a crazy head of hair, and with that mouth, she looks like, I don't know, Angelina Jolie or something. And she doesn't get uptight: she likes to get fucked, she likes to party, I don't know, everything . . . She had Machi wrapped around her finger.

And that's where I wanted to be. I mean, all I had ever asked for was some dinners out and a few lines of blow. I wanted better: a new car, a new place, I don't know, aim high, right.

So when the trip to Mar del Plata came up, I didn't think twice, I got it in my head that this was my moment. Colorada's no dummy, she saw it coming. Later on Machi told me what she said: *Let's go by ourselves, what are you gonna invite her for, we'll pick up some other chick once we get there.* But I was talking his ear off about how I wanted to eat Colorada's pussy in front of him, like *just imagine how I'm gonna make her squirm with these purple bangs.* Shit like that, I don't know.

So we take off for Mar del Plata and we arrive three hours later. I was already getting him hot while we were on the road, moaning, putting on a show, I was feeling up Colorada's tits and licking my lips, I don't know. And when we stopped to do a few lines when we were getting close to Atalaya, Colorada went to the bathroom and I took my shot and crawled up into the passenger seat, and as soon as we took off I was touching him while he drove, getting him ready, I don't know.

Right, so that night we go to the casino and we make a little scratch. We're shitfaced when we make it back to the hotel and Machi's popped like two Viagras, not to mention all the coke. He's on fire. Right, so he puts it in Colorada, basically I stick to the sidelines, a little rubbing and touching, I don't know, suck his cock a few seconds, but more than anything I was waiting for my shot. And I didn't have to wait long.

Machi went off to pour a whiskey and I grabbed Colorada around the waist.

Come here, I said to her, *now it's my turn.*

And when he turned around with his whiskey, we were already all over each other, sixty-nining like crazy. I was playing it cool, but it was the first time I was ever with a chick, at first it grossed me out a little bit, but hey, I don't know, you get used to it and it's pretty hot. The problem is I get to a point where I want someone to stick it in me, you know?

Anyway, we go on like that for an hour, licking and fingering each other. And Machi starts jacking off like a madman and drinking his whiskey. And snorting coke. And my nose starts watering.

Until finally he says, *Stop, stop, I feel like I'm gonna have a heart attack, my chest is hurting and my arm's falling asleep.*

That was when I saw the opportunity I was waiting for.

I don't think so, nasty boy, I said to him in the most

sensual voice I could muster. And I went crawling over to my purse.

It's all that coke and Viagra you've been taking, I said as I took out the pink fur handcuffs.

And you've been watching us and jerking off for an hour, I said, crawling over toward him.

But now I'm going to make you sit still for a moment, I said, and cuffed his hands behind the chair while I knelt between his legs, letting my bangs tickle his dick.

Besides, a heart attack would have put the other arm to sleep, nasty boy, I said before I put his dick in my mouth.

16

PATRÓN CASAL had gotten a contract to take over as director of football down in Peru. After more than two years' experience with his beloved Central and a couple of tries on the home turf in Vélez and Colón, the gig with Deportivo Espejo popped up. It was the perfect opportunity to play in the big leagues. And the money was right, too, way more than they'd offered him to go back to Central, which was his other option.

Everyone who worked at El Imperio heard him finalize the details. It was around midnight, we'd ended our dinner with whiskey and cigars, Machi had promised us after-dinner trim, then Patrón Casal's cell phone rings.

"Excuse me," he says, "I need to take a call."

And we all heard the other people offer toasts and laugh at the roughnecks' table Machi had set up to celebrate.

"If we make it to the quarterfinals, I want to do something special for all the guys," Casal said, "and if we beat Libertadores, we're talking half a mil extra."

The Peruvians from Deportivo Espejo said yes to

everything. They were committed to getting a coach with a strong personality and a killer instinct, and they were backed by the ample cash the Montesinos family had to launder.

"It's done," Casal said when he returned to the rough-necks' table—Carlitos Pairetti was there, Bamba, Tito Mariani, Marcos Feldman, Alejandro Wilkinson—and every one of us saw them toasting and clapping him on the back to congratulate him. And after midnight we heard Mr. Machi say, in all that cigar smoke, over the clinking of whiskey tumblers, how happy he was for his cousin.

And he repeated *my cousin* several times, though we knew he was just first cousin to Machi's wife, Mirta, and Machi, in any case, was more a motorsports man. He could probably tell you the times for every one of Fontanita's races or all the stories about Pairetti in the *Orange Thunder*, but he couldn't give a fuck about soccer. Boxing, sure, he had a little side business there.

But obviously, having big shots like Patrón or Bamba around was good for El Imperio. Soccer and tango. Tango and motorsports. Power and tango. Tango and whores. Those were the reasons for the guests, the reiterated toasts, the interminable after-dinner chitchat.

After a while the table got even rowdier and started ordering champagne.

"Don't forget to tell the media this is where you worked out the contract, cousin," we heard Mr. Machi say.

"Bamba, you can mention it next time you're on TV," Feldman added slyly.

They were on their third round of champagne when we heard Mr. Machi propose one last toast.

"To my cousin—what am I saying!—to my brother from another mother, Eugenio Casal," he said. Moved, or else drunk, El Patrón embraced him.

"You don't know how happy I am," Mr. Machi said, hugging him back. And that must have been true. Soon enough, that very same Saturday, all of us at El Imperio found out though.

At four in the afternoon, Patrón Casal took off for Peru. Three hours hadn't passed when we saw his wife, Claudia, a beautiful woman with ivory-white skin, show up with Mr. Machi and take the stairs up to his office. And if there was anyone who'd managed to ignore her moans and his panting for an hour, well, when the phone rang in reception afterward, the gossip spread through the place like a trail of gunpowder. Eduardo, another hanger-on from the family, picked up. A thirty-year-old nitwit, a good-for-nothing nephew, his sister's kid, Mr. Machi keeps him around doing odd jobs.

"Send me up a bottle of Luigi Bosca, chop-chop," Mr. Machi ordered.

And maybe Eduardo, a spoiled little pushover who can't keep his trap shut, went up there a little too quick.

Because then we found out—we couldn't not find out—that when the bottle of wine reached the office, Mr. Machi still had his shirt unbuttoned over his quivering chest, that Claudia Casal's back—as she lay there facedown on the desk—was glimmering with drops of sweat, and that a pair of pink fur handcuffs were still wrapped around her ivory-white wrists.

17

HOW MANY TIMES had he told his father, his godfather Alejandro, his uncle Carlos, that he wasn't like them.

The little shit believes in love, the three of them joked, with giggles all around, and Alan blushed and said it wasn't that, they didn't understand, it didn't matter. They would never understand.

"I'm not like you," he repeated, biting his lips with irritation, "I don't need the same things you people do."

"Say what you want," Alejandro Wilkinson told him that Christmas, when he was just four months away from turning fifteen, "but it's a done deal: your next birthday you're getting three of the finest hookers Argentina can offer."

"I'll talk with Mariela," Pairetti added.

"I'll cover the tab," Mr. Machi concluded.

And they laughed, the three of them, when Alan repeated that they didn't understand him.

"Okay, fine, we'll go to dinner then," they said to calm him down.

And the night before Alan's birthday, they stopped by the boxing gym where he trained—he hits like a mule, Mr. Machi boasted—and they told him they had a table reserved at the restaurant in the Fajina hotel. A man's dinner, they said. And Alan enjoyed everything until the dessert came.

"Coffee?" Mr. Machi asked. All three—the birthday boy, his godfather, and his so-called uncle—said yes. They talked about boxing for a while.

"I already told you, Alan, in boxing, the big bucks go to the promoters and the bookies," Alejandro said. "You don't believe me, ask your old man."

They all laughed, even Alan, who didn't get the joke.

And when they'd finished their round of coffees and started in on the whiskey, Mariela Báez's yellow Hyundai Galloper showed up, and the diva stepped out with three other girls. The dessert to the dessert. The birthday present. As promised.

"My God, Luis, look how big this boy's getting," Mariela said to Mr. Machi by way of greeting.

Let's talk about Mariela Báez. Her fifteen minutes of fame lasted a decade—the nineties—from her debut on a Sunday talk show to her getting fat to the death of her boyfriend. Her first time on the small screen was in the "Goddess of the Beach" feature on Mariano Trossini's show *Summer Rhythm*. That introduction summed up Mariela's entire career: ass, tits, a huge mouth, and beguiling eyes.

For three and a half minutes or so they would show her: first strolling down the beach with two white sarongs, one tied around her waist and the other around her chest, in marked contrast with her jet-black hair; then in a green thong, her hands barely covering her bare breasts, while Trossini and his chorus of mental defectives made comments like "She's got a great future in front of her," stressing the words *in front of her* as the waves pounded Mariela's grand tumescent breasts.

Later, she made the rounds of every third-rate comedy with a role for a bimbo *au naturel* and a good number of variety shows to boot. In '97 she hooked up with a dance-hall singer named Ramiro. Then her career took a brief musical turn and she even recorded a CD.

"This is the bam-cha-ka, this is the rhythm of love," Mariela sang, and swayed her hips.

But in June of 2000, at the height of his career, Ramiro flipped his truck and died on the way back from a concert.

It was a tough blow for Mariela. She went to the USA to mourn, and when she returned, she found her day had passed and she couldn't get a job in media. Little by little, she started representing other girls: dancers, strippers, escorts.

Now, somewhere in her thirties, she was a kind of madam at a club called Show Business and the main purveyor of kittens at all price points for El Imperio.

"They've got a little present for you," she said, stroking the teenager's cheek. "They're gonna give it to you upstairs."

"No. Papa, tell me you didn't," Alan said.

The three girls giggled. The three men, too. Mariela caressed Alan again and asked him if he didn't like the girls she'd brought him. Like some flesh-peddling goddess, she'd made them in her own image. They were different versions of her, fifteen years younger. Besides their hair color, little distinguished them from what Mariela had been in her heyday on Trossini's show: the same curves, the provocative stare, the same big mouth and beguiling eyes, one after another.

"It's not that," Alan dissimulated.

"Don't worry, they aren't your present, they're just going to give you your present," his papa said, trying to calm him down. "This is the present," he said, and handed a package to one of the girls.

But when Alan and the three girls were about to go up to the bedroom, Mr. Machi leaned in toward the one he had given the package.

"You better drain every drop out of him, got it?" he said with a mischievous wink.

"Don't you worry," the girl answered, hanging back while Mr. Machi patted her ass, "everything will come out . . . just fine."

But not everything came out just fine, because half

an hour later, Alejandro Wilkinson, Carlitos Pairetti, and Mr. Machi saw Alan come down in one of the elevators, alone. They saw his red eyes and pursed lips. They set down their glasses of cognac and their Montecristo cigars and watched him run off and hug another young man— thin and blond—who was waiting for him by the door, and who stroked his head as they embraced. They could read the lips of the thin, blond boy: it's nothing, it's over, everything will be fine. And seconds later, after their embrace went limp like a badly tied knot, Alan came back to the table, and everyone heard the dull thud of the pink fur handcuffs falling on its surface, and Alan saying, "Papa, I think these are yours."

18

"IF I MAY, SIR," Gladis said, entering the bedroom with the breakfast tray.

The lady of the house had gone to Santa Fe again, to spend some time at her parents', as she did every time she and the man of the house fought; the daughter, Luciana, had been living with her boyfriend for several months now; and Alan, the baby, well, the young man, really, had spent the night with one of his little friends. It was now or never.

"Anything else, sir?" Gladis asked, hoping her message was clear, looking intently and shamelessly at the silk sheets concealing Mr. Machi's nakedness and leaving the tray—coffee, toast, strawberry jam—on the bedside table.

"Sugar," Mr. Machi said, "don't forget the sugar . . ."

"Two?" Gladis asked, smiling with her perfect teeth, leaning over to scoop in one spoonful of sugar for each of the protuberances exposed to Mr. Machi's view by the low-cut neckline of her uniform, her lack of a bra, and her posture over the nightstand.

She's a looker, this little Paraguayan, he thought, she's putting it all out there.

Nice tits, nice legs on this bunny.

Gladis turned around to leave and, as was to be expected, dropped something so she could bend over to look for it.

Nice ass too, Mr. Machi confirmed.

"Come here," he said. "I don't want to have breakfast alone, have a seat here." He patted the mattress with his hand.

"Here, sir?" Gladis asked, feigning unease.

"Here?" she asked again, passing her hand over the silk sheets, as though absentmindedly, to the place where she presumed Mr. Machi's sex was waiting.

"Ay, sorry," she said, with a blush that was phonier than a three-dollar bill.

"What will the lady say?" she added.

"The lady isn't home," Mr. Machi said, smacking his lips, as Gladis, already half nude, slipped beneath the sheets. "And I don't like to have breakfast alone. I can't stand being by myself, you know?"

She was a feisty one, the Paraguayan. She shouted loud, mixing Spanish and Guaraní, she scratched, she bit. Mr. Machi liked this scrappy little thing, the way she up and climbed into his bed, almost like she owned it. He liked her enough that he got the urge to try to tame her.

"Get over here," he ordered.

He took her from behind. His heart rate sped up as his hips slapped her buttocks. Face pressed into the pillow, hands shackled to the bedstead by the furry pink handcuffs, Gladis shivered and moaned.

Mr. Machi relished that groaning and the smack of his hips against her buttocks; the furious pumping of his heart echoed in his head like a charging cavalry. Maybe that's why he didn't hear the car pull up, or the tinkle of the keys, or the unmistakable clicking of heels. All he heard—amid moaning, smacking, and thuds—was the sound of the suitcase dropping to the floor.

Then he heard—"In my own bed"—the voice of his wife, who had come back from Santa Fe. "Son of a bitch."

PART VI

FANTASTICAL

19 HIS DOUBTS FAN OUT, stir up the fetid air full of familiar names, unconsidered possibilities. Mr. Machi finds potential enemies where before he had seen only rivals, nuisances, underlings.

Still, there's something that doesn't add up. Which of those enemies lurking in the shadows could organize, let alone execute, a plan like this? Stealing his car, resetting the odometer, taking his Glock and shooting some guy in the face with it, then chaining him up in the trunk with the same pair of handcuffs he used for his sexual high jinks? Not only does Pereyra not know about the fur handcuffs, he would never go in for something so convoluted: he'd just pop a bullet in Machi, end of story. And for the rest: who has the power, the brains? Whoever it was, they couldn't have done it alone. There had to be someone else involved.

But again: who?

And how?

Maybe they paid off that nameless gorilla who watches the garage at El Imperio?

Maybe they paid off Cesspit?

Unless, conjectures Mr. Machi, and every door he opens leads to new layers of confusion and dread, they took the BMW while he was at home? El Barrio has private security, sure, but they could have bribed one of the guards. Or maybe it was someone they'd never suspect. Someone close to him. A family member, for example.

He needs to make sure the handcuffs weren't just a coincidence, something left there without thinking. The stiff is in the trunk of his car, okay. That could just mean that, one way or another—say, if the gorilla was in the mix—the culprits got access to the cars in the El Imperio garage. Offing the guy with Mr. Machi's weapon didn't necessarily make it personal: maybe whoever stole the BMW and reset the odometer(!)—wonder if they brought the stiff from somewhere far away?—knew the Glock was in the glove box, and that was the whole reason they took the car. Maybe it was just a question of opportunity and none of it had anything to do with him, Mr. Machi thinks, and he holds on to that idea.

Until he comes back to the handcuffs . . .

He doesn't remember them being in the BMW. He thinks he left them in the desk drawer at home. But he can't trust his recollections just now. He's nervous, he feels hemmed in, stuck in a dream or some other kind of irreality. But the stink of his own vomit tells him it's real.

Where? Mr. Machi asks himself.

Who? he asks himself.

He asks himself how.

And why.

Last of all, Mr. Machi, a businessman above all else, can't stop wondering: What did they expect to get out of planting a body in his trunk?

Enough, he thinks then, like a person switching off a motor that's running hot and is about to blow; he sets aside his doubts, goes through the contacts in his cell phone, and dials home. He calls without thinking it through.

"*Hola.*" His wife's voice comes through, resonant of several glasses of whiskey, an early-morning Xanax, various cigarettes.

"Mirta," Mr. Machi says, "I need you to go into the drawer in my—"

But the woman interrupts him: "Where are you?"

"I'll tell you later. I need you to look—"

"I'm asking you, where are you, Luis?" the woman interrupts him again.

"Not now, Mirta, this is important. I need—"

"I don't give a fuck, Luis," the woman says, on the offensive. "You woke me up, you made me cook you breakfast, and you said you were on your way. Now where are you?"

Behind her voice he hears the grating of a lighter, a short puff, and then silence as, almost certainly, a curtain of blue smoke rises in front of the woman's face.

"Look, Mirta, we're in the middle of some shit right now."

"I'm not in the middle of anything," the woman says.

"This is serious, Mirta. I wouldn't call you if there was any other way to take care of this. Now shut up and hear me out: I need you to go to my desk and—"

But the woman realizes she's holding the reins for once and she's not about to let them go.

"I'm not in the middle of anything," she repeats, followed by a long, nervous drag, "and if you don't tell me where you are, Luis, I'm hanging up, period."

"I don't know where the fuck I am, Mirta. I need you to focus on—" Mr. Machi is nearly screaming when he hears the click.

Click.

She hung up on me, he thinks. The bitch hung up on me.

The one time I need her to listen and she hangs up on me.

The one time.

Bitch, he thinks.

He asks himself who he can call to find out if the fur handcuffs are at home. With Mirta off the list, and since Alan hasn't spoken to him in months, he doesn't have many options left.

What about calling Eduardo and telling him to go to the house? he wonders. But he knows he's not going to do it. Because for that dipshit to make it to his house from the apartment Mr. Machi rents him next to El Imperio will take at least an hour, and he's got to ditch the thing in the trunk before then, whether or not the handcuffs are his.

But where? Mr. Machi asks himself.

Who? he asks himself.

He asks himself how.

And why.

Never, not even once, amid the avalanche of questions piling up in his mind, has it occurred to him to wonder who the dead man is.

Enough, he finally decides, I'll figure it all out later, right now I'm going to buy a saw and get this over with. And he spits on the floorboard.

20 ONCE AGAIN HE'S passing through those indistinguishable suburban streets, drawing attention to himself, he realizes, leaving witnesses, but he can't find a way out of that interminable dreamlike maze, the downward spiral he was sucked into as soon as he blew a tire on the BMW and walked around to the trunk and looked. If he knew what one was, he would think of a Möbius strip.

Though the vacant lot where he vomited earlier would be perfect, he knows if he buys the saw near there, he won't be able to go back and dump the body. He's got to buy the saw in one place and get rid of the thing in another, somewhere far away.

Where?

Mr. Machi, who's not used to hesitating, who rarely faces questions, feels there's no bottom to the pit he's fallen into.

He circles through those nameless unmarked streets. How do you find your way if every house, every tree, every corner, even every dog that barks as you pass is identical? How do you find a hardware store without asking? He can't just keep going, adding more and more witnesses to the list—especially if, as he drives, his attention isn't focused on finding the store, but on figuring out how things came to this?

Could it be he's confused, and the handcuffs were in the car, forgotten after some one-night stand? Could it be, was there the slightest chance that it was actually a second pair, just like his, chaining up the faceless dead guy in his trunk, purely by coincidence? If Mr. Machi knew it, he would think of the word *probabilistics*.

What's happening to me is weird, and it would be even weirder to think that all this was just down to chance, he thinks. Yet, weirder still is the thought that there's a plot against me.

Why? What's the point? He presses on with the questions to evade the phantom whisper in his ear that tells him this is no chain of coincidences, that someone put that thing in his trunk because they wanted to fuck him up good.

A sign with green letters—GARÓFALO BROTHERS HARDWARE—pulls him away from these questions that suck away at him like ticks. The BMW's tires squeal when he hits the breaks. Mr. Machi emerges without cutting the engine or closing the door. He's already almost inside, a whirlwind, when—to the astonishment of the older woman waiting behind the counter, who's gawking at him, looking like one more piece of furniture—he turns on his heels, kills the motor, locks his car.

The last thing I need is someone stealing it, he thinks. Someone stealing it again.

Now, standing at the counter, he says hello and asks for a saw.

"I got to cut a chain," he says.

"My kid's bicycle chain," he feels obliged to add.

The older woman introduces herself. Says her name is Susana. Susana Garófalo, she says. Same as the name of the store. Her brother, the one with his name on the sign, is asleep, she says. She asks if he's got the bicycle with him, or, if not, where it is. If she could take a look at the chain, maybe she could tell him which saw was best.

"You're not from 'round here, are you, sir?" she asks. She doesn't trust him. Or so it seems to Mr. Machi.

"Look, Ms. Garófalo," he starts to say. The Versace sunglasses that obscure his gaze make him seem even more distant to her.

"Susana, please," she says, this old bag who may have once been a woman and not a furnishing in a hardware store on the outskirts of town.

"Susana," Mr. Machi concedes, impatient to make his purchase and leave, trying to keep his impatience under wraps, "the chain's not too thick, but it's tough . . . just give me the best saw you've got, okay? How much?"

"I can see money's not an issue for you, Señor . . .

what'd you say your name was?" The woman is feeling him out.

Mr. Machi wavers between irritation and horror, and the first, helped along by impatience, triumphs. "I didn't say, Ms. Susana. Now would you be so kind as to give me the saw? I'm in a little bit of a rush," says Mr. Machi, pulling out his wallet.

"Ms.?" the older woman says. "I'm not your grandmother. You can call me Susana."

Then, stepping fully into her role as salesperson, she continues: "I said the thing about the money because I saw your car and I imagined a man in your position might be interested in a Whave chain cutter I have. It's not the cheapest option, but—"

"Give it to me," Mr. Machi says, cutting off any opportunity for dialogue, then pays and dashes out with the box—emblazoned with white letters forming the word *Whave*—under his arm.

Wherever he ends up dropping the body, he decides, it better be as far from that bitch as possible.

He gets into the BMW, puts it in gear, takes off, and retraces his route back to the Panamericana: a black bolt of lightning crossing the filthy asphalt once more. Only forty minutes have passed.

21 MR. MACHI heads back and reaches the Acceso Oeste. He drives and drives, not thinking of anything, just letting himself go. As if being there behind the wheel—the supple leather he selected himself, the dull roar of the motor, the relaxing route—makes all the rest of it disappear, puts everything back into place. As if driving his two-hundred-thousand-dollar car creates a parallel universe, one without dead bodies whose faces have been torn to pieces by a bullet.

Exit signs flit past, one after the other—ITUZAINGÓ, PADUA, MERLO—and Mr. Machi drives on without thinking, free for the moment from worries or fears. But the illusion is fragile. Anything could shatter it. And something does, inevitably. A trifle. There's a quiver in the pocket of his Scappino suit, and Mr. Machi takes a moment to realize it's his cell phone, not ringing, just vibrating, one, two, three times. The questions come back into his head—who, how, why—along with uncertainty and the desperate urge to get rid of it. That thing.

A few minutes later, the pocket of the Scappino vibrates again.

Who the motherfucking fuck is it now, Mr. Machi thinks, hands on the wheel and eyes on the road. Somehow he knows it can only be bad news. More bad news.

But what? he wonders.

And why is his phone vibrating instead of ringing? he wonders, trying to take cover in mundane conundrums the same way, seconds before, he did in the graceful handling of the BMW.

MORENO.

Again. The vibration returns, one, two, three times.

LA REJA.

I know my way around here. Old Man Heredia's gym was out here, Mr. Machi recalls, and Coco Noriega's place was a little farther on.

Coco Noriega, he thinks, long time since I saw him. That's a relationship to cultivate, a tie worth strengthening. When I get out of this shit I'll send him a couple of invites to El Imperio for next week, Mr. Machi decides. Those government contacts, one or two in every administration, have been as valuable as any other deal I've made these past twenty-two years, he gloats. I gotta admit, Alejandro Wilkinson was right about that.

"You need friends in politics, Luis, now more than ever," he told him in November of '83, when Mr. Machi opened the Skylight with the insurance money from the bar, just before he changed the name of the place to El Imperio. "Guys like me, like Almirón, like Romero, we aren't enough anymore."

"But you're a friend," Mr. Machi protested. And he meant it.

"That's not what I'm saying," Wilkinson answered. "I know we're friends, real friends, not people who take advantage of each other. But cops, even army guys, they aren't going to do the trick anymore. We're facing down years and years of constitutional democracy. The rule of law, get it? Trust me, you'll need new allies."

And so it was. With the patience of a goldsmith, as the years went by, Mr. Machi did everything he had to do to get those people in his pocket. He even pursued what Alejandro Wilkinson would have called *symbolically valuable* friendships with guys like Rodolfo Schenkler. When Rodolfo got out of the pen after serving a sentence for killing his father, then re-created himself as the lawyer in charge of the most prestigious human rights organization in the country, Mr. Machi made sure the man was a frequent guest at El Imperio.

So, guys like that: congressmen, ministers, secretaries, lobbyists.

It was thanks to these contacts that he heard in advance about certain devaluations, and got his slice of a number of ancillary ventures in healthcare in the early days of the democracy, buying low and selling high to the state throughout the nineties; thanks to them, he got his money out just days before the *corralito*; thanks to them, he managed to keep working despite the laws and ordinances they'd been ramming up his ass ever since all those little shits got burned to a crisp at that rock show in Once, even though the fire exits and emergency systems in El Imperio couldn't pass a routine inspection.

Just a phone call away: Coco Noriega, Drommo the engineer, a couple of mayors from the outlying towns, some Sushi Boys, Thaelman—who isn't only the new chief of government, but also the owner of the Garret, the nightclub across from El Imperio—and last but not least, two guys from the Hernández clan—the ones who really held the reins. Every one of them is in his address book.

But the three persistent pulses from his phone pull him out of his reflections and remind Mr. Machi that he's alone and that no phone call can get him out of this.

He cuts the wheel brusquely and exits the interstate. He veers left and follows the curve, passing the beer distributor, and after that the cemetery. He crosses the train tracks and goes a bit farther. Past the soap factory, he turns onto a dirt road. His cell vibrates again, and Mr. Machi wearily takes it from his suit pocket and tosses it into the passenger seat. The phone thuds against the green box with the word *Whave* spelled out in white. The two objects—chain cutter and phone—conjure the image of the handcuffed cadaver in the trunk. Relentless as winter, the urge returns to know for sure whether the pink fur cuffs are his or not.

He decides to call Marcos Feldman, who lives in El Barrio, too, just a few houses away from him, and ask him to go have a look. That way, he'll be able to avoid talking to his wife and facing any uncomfortable questions.

Mr. Machi upbraids himself for not thinking of this before. I won't have to explain anything to Marcos, he'll think it's just some bullshit I'm caught up in.

And so he parks on the dirt road and picks up the phone, which just then goes back to vibrating. One, two, three times. On the screen, which is blank, several gray lines quiver with each vibration. Mr. Machi pushes the button that should take him to the menu. Nothing. The screen's still blank.

He tries again.

Nothing.

One more time.

Nothing.

Frantically, he pushes every button, still with the same result.

Nothing.

He can't even shut it down.

What next? he asks the gods, letting his head drop against the seatback in resignation.

Did they hack my phone? he asks himself afterward, resignation giving way to fear.

In response, the phone vibrates. One, two, three times.

No, no way, he decides then, and shakes his head, dismissing the idea. It must be some problem with my service, he thinks, or else I damaged it when I threw it against the box. Who do I think I'm up against? The KGB? The CIA?

If he knew what MI6 was, Mr. Machi would have thought of them, too.

No, he shakes his head again, and a person who hours before thought he had no enemies at all now thinks to himself, I don't have enemies *that* powerful.

The main thing is to figure out what's the deal with the handcuffs, he repeats to himself. If they're mine, cutting the chain's not enough, I need to get them off his wrists. Or burn the body. Why not.

He shakes his head again, rejecting the idea as excessive. Not that. Fire, no. That's the last thing he needs. Fire is a terrible idea, even if it is hygienic. It would draw even more attention. He looks at the green box with the white letters and curses.

Senile old bitch, he says, punching the box and thinking about the hardware store; she sold me this shit and what do I know, maybe I don't even need a chain cutter. Or maybe what I need is a hacksaw. To cut through the dead guy's wrist.

A deep nausea halts this train of thought. The mere idea of it makes him sick, and for the fourth time in minutes, he shakes his head. Mr. Machi imagines blood, bits of flesh and fat and more blood. A shiver like a frightened mouse runs down his spine, and he can feel his nausea wavering between his chest and throat.

Before I do anything, I need to know if those cuffs are mine, he concludes, restraining the urge to vomit.

I need to call Marcos.

Then his cell vibrates, one, two, three times, the screen still blank, and Mr. Machi realizes that without his cell, he's got no contacts, and without his contacts, he's left with the only two numbers he knows by heart: El Imperio and his home.

He puts the BMW in gear and goes looking for a pay phone. His mind traces out a picture of his wife grinning, her glass of whiskey and her cigarette in front of her.

Mr. Machi swallows his hatred without savoring it, the way you swallow medicine.

22

HE FINDS A service station across from a call shop and parks his BMW alongside the first pump.

"Fill her up, I'll be right back," he says to the kid in the red uniform who comes over to attend to him.

"You want us to squeegee the windows?" the kid in the red uniform asks.

"Did I say anything about the windows?" Mr. Machi replies, and commands him, without waiting for an answer, "Fill her up and don't touch anything, I'll be right back."

"Yes, sir. Sorry, sir." The kid in the red uniform says in a tone Mr. Machi has heard many times, and which he once more mistakes for respect when it's barely even contempt. Then he crosses the street.

"Use booth two," the fat chick behind the counter tells him.

Mr. Machi enters the booth with the numeral 2 scrawled on the poorly washed glass, dials his home number, and hears his wife's voice.

"Hello."

"Mirta, it's me," Mr. Machi says. "I need you to go—"

"Sure, sure . . . you got a lot of balls, I'll tell you that," she says, raising her voice and following up with a laugh. "Might I be permitted to know where my husband is at present?"

"In a call shop in La Reja, close to Moreno, where Coco Noriega's place is, remember? Near Old Man Heredia's gym," Mr. Machi says, and another disturbing idea, or rather, the embryo of a disturbing idea, begins to gestate in his mind.

Noriega, he thinks, Heredia. He thinks of one guy shot in the face, of another guy shot in the face. He thinks of a letter. Of the muffled voice of Old Man Heredia saying this time he'd done it, he'd never forgive him for this. But there's no time for that now. His wife didn't expect an answer, and the shock of getting one leaves her speechless. He knows if he lets her react, she'll ask him what he's doing there, so he takes advantage of the brief silence.

"Now, please, listen to me: I need you to go to my desk and look and see if the fur handcuffs, the pink ones, are in the drawer," Mr. Machi says before his wife has the chance to respond.

"Are you crazy, Luis? How can you ask me to do that? Isn't it enough that . . . ?" And for the first time, his wife's tone of voice isn't feigned, for the first time in three calls that day, the indignation and surprise are real. "Who are you planning on fucking now that you need me to look for them?"

There is a silence. Neither of them fills it with words. Then the woman sobs.

"How far are you going to push me, Luis, how far?"

"Mirta," Mr. Machi says.

"I'm going, Luis, I'm going to my parents' place in Santa Fe, and this time—"

"I know, I know, Mirta: this time, it's forever," Mr. Machi finishes her sentence, exasperated.

Then he says, doing everything he can to keep himself from screaming, to cut the bullshit, they both know she's not going anywhere, and if she does, she'll be back in three or four days, and this time it doesn't have anything to do with a girl; she needs to stop thinking about that bimbo from Paraguay and listen up. He's in a bind, a big one, and he needs her to go to the desk and . . .

She's sobbing again. The sorrow wells up inside her and spills over and it somehow brings a serenity neither whiskey nor tranquilizers could ever give her. She feels sad, but in a romantic way. She is humiliated, and in her humiliation realizes she still retains a bit of self-respect. She talks again. This time, her voice is calm.

"No, Luis, no," she says.

"If you want to say goodbye, you'd best be here in fifteen minutes," she says.

"After that I'm leaving," she says. "Forever."

"Your breakfast will be in the kitchen," she says.

"Don't try and find us, you sack of shit, not me and not Alan either," she says.

And she hangs up.

Fuck, Mr. Machi thinks. And hangs up in turn. If he knew who Kurt Gödel was, he'd think of the incompleteness theorems.

The best thing, he decides, is to buy a hacksaw. A fine-tooth hacksaw.

PART VII

WILD

DOGS

23 THEY FOUND BULLDOG'S BODY in a house in the William C. Morris neighborhood nine days after his death.

The crack of the shotgun didn't make them call the police. No one in William Morris calls the cops for a thing like that. The smell, either: a little stench, a rat or two, none of that's going to faze anyone. In William C., as the residents like to call it, no one calls the cops for anything, truth be told.

But after a week, there was no questioning the fetor emerging from the house, and by the ninth day, the comings and goings of the vermin had gotten to be too much, even for the residents of William C. So someone kicked in the wooden door and then, yes, the cops had to be called.

The shotgun, sawed off to make the job easier, was lying there next to the body. The dirt floor had soaked up most of the blood, leaving an enormous dark blotch that resembled a map of Brazil.

Thanks in part to the rats, but mostly to the sawed-off shotgun with its sixteen-gauge shells, Bulldog's face had disappeared in a crater of blood, brains, and splintered bones. Still there to identify him were the tattoo on his right shoulder and the scars on his back, mementos from the beatings his father had dealt him in his boyhood, back when they still called him Little Hugo.

On the table lay a note. The people who saw it say that it was spattered with remnants of Bulldog's face.

I hope you forgive me Mr. Eredia, it supposedly said. *I no I faled you but that guy punched like a mule.*

Plus I lost my legs, it supposedly went on.

I no I shudn't have gone with those hookers at Mr. Machi's the other nite but you no how it goes, the note said, supposedly.

And supposedly he finished by saying, *You told me strait out an opportunity like this one u just get once in your life. So Im done.*

I hope you forgive me, Mr. Eredia, he repeated.

24 HE RESTED HIS ELBOW on the mat and shook his head. A cold, metallic sweat rolled down from the nape of his neck. More than anything, he saw lights: red lights, yellow, and a few extremely fine rays of bluish green. He looked around, trying to find something to focus on, and his eyes played games with him, doubling and smudging everything.

Nothing.

The faces in disarray and the cameras faded menacingly, a brunette in white seemed to have four tits, one bald head split into two.

Lights, lights, shouting, lights.

Finally, with some effort, he managed to make out an arm swinging toward him, and a face.

And the numbers: three, four, five.

He stopped, trying to look composed, and almost managed to do so, despite his glassy eyes, his wayward gaze.

Six, seven.

Then he started, bit by bit—first one foot, then the

other—to dance back and forth, trying to remember what round it was.

Eight.

The little bald man in the sky-blue shirt stopped the standing eight count, and as he grabbed the fighter's hands in their twelve-ounce Corti gloves, he asked if he could keep going.

Martínez bit his mouth guard, nodded his head yes, and remembered: round five.

He rode it out as best he could and tried to stay off the ropes, keeping to the center of the ring. He even got in a few good ones before the bell sent him back to his corner.

"Don't sweat it, kid. If we don't give up, we can beat this guy," his corner man said to encourage him. A giant man with thick gray hair, yellow teeth, and a nose that spoke of a lifetime of liver shots and KOs.

Heredia—that was his name—smeared Vaseline on his right eyebrow and continued: "Box him, fend him off with the left, and when you hit him, hit him good."

"We're gonna box him," he continued, reverting to the first-person plural. "That's what we're best at, and that's where this guy is weak."

When he was done with the Vaseline, he put the mouth guard back in and repeated, "We're gonna box him." But while he spoke to the fighter, he scanned the ringside seats for a face.

Martínez nodded without looking at Heredia, promising himself that when the fight was over he'd break his dick off in that brunette holding the signboard with the number six over her head. Those whores from Don Luis's place the night before had left him itching for more.

Bell.

The sixth round was quick and easy, much like the first four—like they should be, Heredia thought from his corner—with Martínez getting in the best shots and Santos, the kid from Tucumán, trying in vain to come after him.

Maybe it was just a scare, Heredia thought.

Calmer now, almost as if the knockdown had been a bad joke, he greeted Martínez with a smile, sponging down his face. Heredia told him to keep going like that, fend the kid off with the left and don't punch unless you're sure you'll hit the mark.

"Like that, we can beat him on points," Heredia said, and rinsed his face again, thinking less about the remaining rounds than the next bout, their odds for the title, his first champion pupil.

The brunette came out with a poster reading seven, and when she passed Martínez, she winked and gave him a smile that could make your dick turn to granite. Her dress had a long slit that showed off her left leg, and its generous neckline gave a generous view of her more than generous cleavage. She was a little too made up, and she had a ravenous look about her, hungry for a chance that would probably never come.

At first, the seventh went just like the round before:

Martínez stuck to the center of the ring and held Santos, the kid from Tucumán, at bay for two and a half minutes.

Until he slipped up.

Then Santos saw an opening and threw a murderous series of combos: hooks, jabs, crosses. Heredia got nervous and started to sweat.

This is a dirty business, he told himself, as if he'd only just found out, as if he'd only gotten into pro fighting the day before. I told Machi to bring me a tomato can, just a few more fights and we'd be up for the title, instead he gives me this brute—he interrupted himself to shout at Martínez to get out of there, to throw the left—this brute with lead fists, and either nobody told this kid it wasn't his time yet, or else they did tell him and he got here and saw the lights and the packed stands, the TV cameras and the trim, and decided, "To hell with it, I'm gonna play Rocky."

Bell.

"Take it easy, don't go out there like it's kill or be killed, that's just playing his game. We're gonna go out there and box and we'll take him on points," Heredia repeated.

"Be careful, dammit," he growled.

The brunette came out with a big eight on her signboard, and Martínez didn't even look at her.

Both fighters reached the center of the ring certain this would be the last round: Santos was losing on points and had taken the lion's share of the punches, but Bulldog couldn't hold out for three more rounds like the last one. Heredia knew it too: all he needed was to see the two of them stop, to watch them shake their heads on their way out, how they faced off in the center of the ring.

Machi, you cocksucking son of a bitch, he thought. I'll never forgive you for this, he thought.

Hugo Martínez, whom everyone called Bulldog, attacked, giving it everything he had: his soul, his fists, his will, his hunger. The little man with the bald head gave him a warning for a low blow, then another for a headbutt.

It was funny, it seemed like all of a sudden the two men had started to hate each other—they'd never seen each other before, and they'd never see each other again— even if that hatred would dissipate as soon as the fight had ended. It wasn't a sport anymore, it was contempt in its purest form.

And there they were, trading blows as ferocious as they were devoid of technique, when a thud sounded out, brutal, definitive, and—as the cameras showed over and over, from different angles and at different speeds—there was the body falling in defeat.

The little man in the sky-blue shirt could have counted to a hundred, two hundred, a thousand. Even ten thousand.

Nearly fifteen minutes passed until the fallen man, now back in his dressing room, would return to consciousness, in the arms of his coach, and know.

In the meantime, in the dressing room of the winner, the other coach was cackling with a bottle of beer, dripping sweat, in the middle of a group of friends. Listening to a voice on the phone that was putting together the next bout.

"Yeah, I want Morales . . . I told you he couldn't lose . . . In a month, give or take . . . Yeah, Coco, listen to me, work things out with Loco Wilkinson . . . Right, right, I'll call you Wednesday," Mr. Machi said—his pockets bulging with gambling money—just as Santos, the kid from Tucumán, grabbed the brunette's head in the shower, her dress soaking wet and pulled up over her waist, and finished in her mouth.

PART VIII

INCLUDED

IN THE

PRESENT

CLASSIFICATION

25 AT A MINI-MART run by a Chinese family, Mr. Machi finds the hacksaw he needs. He also buys a bag of charcoal, a small bottle of lighter fluid, and a large bottle of Coke. He thinks this makes him look like a regular customer— despite the suit jacket buttoned to the top, the smell of vomit, the splatters of mud—and therefore less memorable.

Again, he sets off in search of an opportune spot— secluded, isolated, unpeopled—where he can get rid of the thing once and for all and put an end to this nightmare. Mr. Machi drives aimlessly, unaware which streets he's already passed through, lost in confusion, fear, and weariness, in the bottomless downward spiral of his own ineptitude. More than anything, he needs a couple of lines of blow—just the thought of it makes a tongue grow from his nose and start licking its lips.

Okay, let's get a grip, he says to himself. We're going to make a list of possible culprits. Forget how they did it. Forget why. We're going to concentrate on who wants to hurt us. He susses things out like two people in conversation: as though Mr. Machi were talking to Luis, and as if

Luis—given the circumstances—could be someone more than Mr. Machi.

Cesspit, he thinks, to begin with.

He's cold-blooded. I'm the only one who could link him to the kid from Ciudadela, if they were ever to reopen the case. And there's also the thing with Don Rogelio. Plus, Alejandro recommended him, and now that he's dead— goddamn heart attack—maybe Cesspit feels like he doesn't have to worry about betraying me anymore. Okay. But he doesn't know about the fur handcuffs.

Then he thinks of his wife.

There's been a lot of ups and downs over the years. If somebody's fucking her and putting ideas in her head, Mirta's capable of anything. Mr. Machi knows it, he's pushed her into more than a few deviant acts, and she was happy to go along. Reminiscing, he even smiles as the words *capable of anything* flash in his mind.

Now: Patrón Casal, he thinks.

I fucked his wife and if that dipshit Eduardo ran his mouth, then all the boys would have found out. I doubt Patrón would have the balls for something like this, though . . . but then again, Patrón's living in Peru now. Or Colombia. Or Venezuela, what do I know. And down there, a *sicario*'s easy to come by, he thinks. He doesn't really know what the word *sicario* means, but he likes to use it; it sounds lethal, like something from an action flick.

Who else? he asks himself, and turns onto another dirt road.

Thrice he shakes his head no when his son's name comes up on the list. Or the name of his son's boyfriend. Again, he refuses to believe. But he knows it could be. Of course it could be.

A stray dog's barking jerks him out of his ruminations. He slams on the brakes. In front of him, in the middle of an overgrown meadow, a dilapidated, abandoned shack catches his eye.

That's the one, he thinks.

The rusty, broken gate screeches softly when Mr. Machi opens it to pull the BMW inside. Once there, he takes off his Scappino jacket, his Versace sunglasses, and his Rolex, rolls up his Armani sleeves, and opens up the trunk.

Just one more time, he thinks.

26 BETTER GET CRACKING NOW, he tells himself, once inside the abandoned property. He thinks in shorter and shorter sentences because doing so gives him the sense it'll be easier to keep his revulsion under control.

He shortens the initial phrase: Get cracking now.

Cut, he thinks, and detach.

A mechanical task.

Impersonal.

Clean.

Like sawing through a board.

Or a piece of furniture.

Or a badly made doll, now worse for wear.

Get cracking, he repeats, again truncating the phrase, but when he grazes the corpse's stiffened arm, his entire body contracts with a jerk that combines nausea and terror and uncontrollable shaking.

I need to get my mind on something else, Mr. Machi knows, bending over at the waist. And he reverts to his telegraph-style thinking.

Imagine, he thinks.

Come up with hypotheses.

Distance yourself from what you're doing.

Avoidance, he thinks.

Manual versus intellectual labor.

He goes back to his list of suspects as he saws through the wrist, as blood and bits of flesh collect on the pink fur of the cuffs.

One of the girls? he asks himself.

Nobody likes to feel abandoned. Even if they know the rules of the game. Colorada? Nah, no way. More likely the other one. She got hung up on the powder something fierce.

"Powder," Mr. Machi repeats aloud, and his nose starts watering.

Or Gladis, he thinks. The first thing she knew the morning we got caught fucking was I had to give her the pink slip and replace her with Herminia. I paid her a good severance, obviously. But with a black bitch, you never know. They got a chip on their shoulder, every last one of them.

The hacksaw snags on bone. Mr. Machi is perspiring and the odor of his sweat mixed with vomit seems to rouse the mosquitoes, which emerge from the meadow in battalions, attacking his neck, his arms, his face.

"Goddamn motherfucker," Mr. Machi says as he kills one, transforming it into a smudge of blood and grime between his hand and neck. And he doesn't know if he's cursing the mosquito, the snagged blade, the cadaver, or himself. He tries to free the hacksaw's teeth from the splintered bone. Scraps of fabric and tendon make the operation more difficult.

And Don Rogelio's kids?

It's true that they did a good job covering up the old man's death—a doctor Mr. Machi paid off chalked it up to cardiac arrest, and then the goons from Doctor Tango came over to work for him—and no one knew Cesspit had been involved. But the information could have gotten out. Same goes for the thing with the mortgage.

I'm getting paranoid, he thinks. Nothing really points to any of them. Or to Heredia. Or Noriega, either. Just because I'm out this way and they popped into my head doesn't mean anything.

"Or does it?" Mr. Machi asks himself aloud, killing the thousandth of a million mosquitoes that are swarming him now like squadrons of Sea Harriers.

The thing is to keep your eyes on the clues.

Signs, he thinks.

Secret codes.

Hidden meanings.

Nothing is just a coincidence, a voice says—the voice of fear—inside Mr. Machi.

Why a blown tire?

What were they trying to say with the caltrops?

And hacking his phone, what's with that? Who do they want to keep him from contacting?

What are they after?

The questions keep piling up. Why today? Does the date mean something?

Mr. Machi realizes he doesn't know what day it is. Fatigue is blunting his memory and his senses.

Signs, he thinks again.

Signs, he repeats, and it's like a revelation.

Then he sets to feverish work, forgetting the mosquitoes eating him for lunch and the disgust he should feel at handling the cadaver. He has to go over it inch by inch. He can't chuck it until he's sure there are no more clues left, nothing else that might point to him, like the handcuffs. Nothing he's overlooked.

27

PROBLEM IS, everything he decides leads him into another predicament. Every answer spawns unforeseen questions. Now he's seesawing. Does he look the body over while it's still in the trunk—it's a squeeze, it's uncomfortable, but it makes for a safer getaway if need be—or does he pull the stiff out, lay it in the meadow, and examine it in detail stretched out on the rocky soil. It's a risk, but Mr. Machi opts for a thorough inspection, and hurries to finish what he has started.

Me, who never cleaned a fish, never gutted a chicken, he thinks, staring nonplussed at the blood and flesh trapped beneath his fingernails. Finally he's done it, the hand pulls away from the arm at the wrist, and they separate—in opposite directions—from the fur handcuffs that remain there, dangling useless from a hinge in the trunk.

Mr. Machi embraces the corpse like a brother and heaves it onto his chest. He feels the dead weight, the stiffness in the muscles, the flop of the faceless head against his shoulder. He drops it in a clearing in the meadow, some ten or twelve feet from the BMW. Then he goes back for the hand and leaves it off to one side, propped against a gray stone.

He pauses a moment to take a deep breath, look down at his work, and suppress his disgust. He glances around, too. This is the peak moment of danger, he thinks. If someone shows up now, he won't have time to react. The fear in Mr. Machi's chest is growing, barely leaving room for revulsion. He walks over to the rusty gate and looks back at his handiwork, calming down when he sees nothing is visible through the overgrown grass.

He goes back to the body and starts his inspection. The scrupulous, blind inspection of a man with no notion of what he hopes to find. He goes through the pockets of the suit, the folds, the cuffs, stretches out the fingers of the other hand, the one still attached to the body, balled up into a fist. He looks at the shoes: soles, tongue, insoles. When he's done studying the suit and the shoes, he strips everything else off. The corpse is naked now except for briefs, socks, and shirt. Mr. Machi studies the man's underclothes. Disgust returns when he sees the shriveled, dead dick. In the breast pocket of the shirt he finds a ballpoint pen, and his fear revives: on the barrel of the pen, in flowing letters, are the name and logo of an early business venture of Mr. Machi's, the predecessor to El Imperio: the Skylight Tango Bar.

Mr. Machi sits next to the corpse—on the ground, hidden by the grass, devoured by mosquitoes—and trembles. He looks into the void and trembles. Without letting go of the ballpoint, which seems, in some twisted and ungraspable way, to incriminate him, he shakes and shivers. Finally he cries, hugging his knees. And shakes some more.

When Mr. Machi has his body back under control, he dries his tears a little and pries open his own clenched fist to slip the pen into the pocket of his Armani.

I can't give up yet, he thinks. He looks at his hands, stained with blood and dirt. I must have left traces all over the clothes that thing is wearing, he thinks. He strips the cadaver of its remaining garments and puts all the clothing in a pile. He folds the socks, the briefs, the shirt, the pants. He's folding the blue blazer when another voice in his head pipes up. As if the faded blue fabric were calling to him, Hey, you and me got some unfinished business. Or something like that. There's a message here, Machi knows, or rather intuits, but what?

He looks again.

What, he asks, what?

He stretches the suit out next to the corpse.

What? Again he looks it over, and then the obvious leaps out at him, the first thing he should have seen: the tag on the suit says MACHITEX.

This'll never end, he thinks.

He multiplies whatever evidence he must have left on

the corpse's clothes by the tag from the factory he used to own and the result is: he's got to burn it.

Burn it, yeah, but not here. So he finishes folding the blazer, sets it with the rest of the clothing, and lays it in the car, as though the trunk of the BMW were a drawer in an armoire. Which he then shuts.

28 BEFORE LEAVING, he picks the hand up off the rock. He looks at it with curiosity, with a kind of scientific distance: he looks at the palm, the knuckles, tries to calculate its age based on the wrinkles in the fingers. For the first time since he found the body, Mr. Machi wonders about the dead man's identity. He compares the dead hand with his own.

Until yesterday, that nude, dead thing had a name. A name he would answer to if someone shouted it in the street. He had his likes and dislikes. A family, friends, memories. He must have enjoyed certain music, certain colors, a certain type of woman. Someone must have loved him. And someone must have wanted to see him end up like he is now. Mr. Machi asks himself if they might have ever met. Either way, he sums things up to himself, laying the hand over the cold, inert torso lying in the grass, he's dead now and I'm alive, so I better hightail it out of here.

Hopefully they won't find you too soon, he thinks, talking to the cadaver. You'd have to start stinking and someone would have to pass by this very spot. Someone who wouldn't just assume it was the stench of some rotten animal, someone curious enough to come over and take a look. But that probably won't happen. With a little luck, I mean. And with even more luck, you'll get eaten by street dogs and that'll be the last anyone sees of you.

Same as when he came in, the busted, rusty gate screeches as Mr. Machi opens it. He gets in the BMW and looks through the window one last time. He makes sure the grass covers the scene. Everything looks normal, even the half-open gate.

"See you 'round, dude," he says aloud, and waits a few seconds for the impossible response before putting the car in first and taking off. A few minutes later and the BMW is crossing the Acceso Oeste like a black bolt of lightning, leaving looks of astonishment and envy in its wake.

The sun shines—unpleasant, overbearing—and Mr. Machi puts his Versaces back on. He feels, in spite of it all, that things are starting to return to normal.

PART IX

THAT

SHAKE

LIKE

MADMEN

29

"WE NEED NAMES, Machi, understand?" Romero had said.

When you saw him, skinny, darkskinned, with a beak like a toucan and greasy curled hair, he didn't look so dangerous. But Mr. Machi, the young Mr. Machi from 1974, knew that yeah, he was dangerous, that there wasn't much distance between showing up in his magazine on a list of the General's enemies and showing up in a trench with a bullet through the nape of your neck. Not much at all.

The best enemy—Romano liked to say, liked to write in *El Caudillo*—is a dead enemy.

"The Fatherland will make it up to you, Machi," he added with a severe expression on his thin, angular face. "We know you're no Peronist and you just took over the factory, plus we never had any problems with your father. And plus we know you guys aren't Reds, or Jews, or internationalist one-world-government types. You hear what I'm getting at, right?"

"One more thing," Inspector Almirón said to him later

on the phone, as if the two conversations were one and the same. "What's good for us is good for your factory. Or do you want another strike like the one in December? How much did you lose on that one, Machi? Wasn't that when Don Luis had his heart attack? Just think . . ."

And though in fact it was an aneurysm and not a heart attack, the young Mr. Machi knew it was true, that the bullshit textile workers' strike was what put his father out of commission and obliged him to step into the king's shoes. He'd had to abandon the comfort of the bar—which his father, Don Luis, now managed—and take over running the factory.

"We're looking for names—people in your factory, at your friends' businesses, names you might know from the bar, from the nightlife. We understand each other, right?" Romero said, and something was slightly menacing in his tone.

"The more you produce, the more money you make," Inspector Almirón's voice chimed in, finishing the thought days later, "and, look, a peaceful society is a productive society, right? With no Reds around fucking things up."

No doubt about it: the best enemy was a dead enemy.

And so, in part for convenience's sake, in part out of fear, the young Mr. Machi scribbled down a few names, six or seven, on a sheet of paper. Class warriors, they called themselves, Trotskyites from the PCT or PRT or God knows what mishmash of letters, and a couple more who called themselves Peronists—we're the Peronist Underground, they said, but they sure seemed like Reds—guys that were making life hard for him. Ball-breakers, not like the union bosses. With those guys, it was easy to make problems go away: a nice fat envelope and basta.

"Communist scum, Machi, you hear me? That's who we want. Rabble-rousers," said Romero—skinny, dark-skinned, with a beak like a toucan—seated in front of him.

"Think it over" were the last words conveyed on the phone by the faceless voice of Inspector Almirón a few days later.

And the young Mr. Machi thought it over. A few names on a piece of paper. That was all: a piece of paper, six or seven names, who cares? The next few days, at the gates to the factory, there were noises, squealing brakes, slamming doors, a gunshot or two. But naturally, no one saw or heard a thing. Weeks later, on a Monday, the factory had to put a notice in the paper looking for workers. And the list of those "brought to justice" appeared in the pages of *El Caudillo*.

When Don Luis started asking questions, the young Mr. Machi told him to stick to worrying about the bar. As for power—it turned out he liked it.

30 "DOLE THEM OUT RIGHT and they'll end up owing you two or three times over," Coco Noriega told him long before he offered him the gig.

"They're a business expense," Alejandro Wilkinson had agreed.

"You rarely do one without an ulterior motive in mind," his father-in-law said.

"And they're not just for friends," his father told him.

Mr. Machi had listened to all of them, at various times, and had taken note of what they had to say. It wasn't often they agreed, and that gave him a lot to think about. So when, in the mid-eighties, he became a stockholder in the Artigas Clinic, partly with his own funds and partly as a front man for Coco Noriega, who was minister of the interior at the time, he decided to put into practice the complex Theory of Favors he had been developing.

Carlos Amante, the line cook, one of his most loyal employees, had a son who was some kind of gimp. A nasty disease, complicated, hard to treat. The first thing Mr. Machi did when he came on at Artigas was tell the guy he could go to the clinic whenever he felt like it, that all he had to do was say Mr. Machi's name and they'd take care of him gratis. He told him he'd heard about the hard times he was going through with his kid's condition, and that El Imperio was one big family.

Now Carlos owed him a favor.

The second thing he did was call Artigas and make it clear that if Carlos Amante went there, they were to tell him sorry, his name wasn't on any list. Let the guy piss and moan, then wait awhile, then call him.

The third thing he did was wait.

Three months later, Carlos Amante's kid had an attack, and they went running to Artigas Clinic. Naturally, when he got there, they told him his name didn't ring a bell, they were very sorry, but they couldn't do anything for him. In the interim, Carlos Amante Junior started to shake and spaz out in the waiting room in his mother's arms.

"Talk to Mr. Machi," Carlos Senior begged, "he's the one who told me, just ask him . . ."

And so after a while, one of the receptionists called Mr. Machi, who told them of course they should take care of Carlos Jr., and to please put his father on the phone.

"I don't know how this happened, Carlos, but don't worry, they'll take care of your kid and the two fuckups that made you wait are fired," Mr. Machi said.

"Thank you, sir, thank you," Carlos Amante babbled.

So now the line cook owed Mr. Machi two favors.

The doctors intervened quickly, but it was too late, and Carloitos suffered serious brain damage. They kept him eight days at the Artigas Clinic with the best care money could buy. Eight days Carlos didn't have to go to work.

"We're a family," Mr. Machi repeated the first night he went to visit. "You can come back when the kid's better."

Now Carlos owed him three favors.

And when the eight days were up and he went back to El Imperio, Mr. Machi had him sent up to the office and told him how much he regretted that the doctors' efforts hadn't been enough. They had to be thankful it wasn't worse. They had to keep looking ahead.

"Where'd your boy work?" he asked.

"In a call center," the father answered, "but now . . ."

"Probably it'll be hard for him to find a job now, no?" Mr. Machi said.

"It occurred to me," he went on, "that we could set him up with something here. Help out in the kitchen, have him wash dishes, something like that."

He clapped him on the back: "Pay won't be much, but at least he'll be with his family."

Carlos Amante thanked him, weeping silently.

Now he owed him four.

"Hey, now, don't cry, just remember: you scratch my back, I scratch yours."

A self-made man, that's me, Mr. Machi thought. And his Theory worked.

31

"A LITTLE CHAT BETWEEN FRIENDS,"
Chamorro had told him.

When they were settled in at one of the tables in the private dining room, Mr. Machi ordered champagne and asked him what the deal was, not bothering to beat around the bush.

Chamorro said his visit was just a sign of his goodwill, of the solid friendship that united them. There'd been some dissatisfaction on the subject of days off, and then about one of the waiters, Pablo, who no longer worked there. A rumor had reached the office that the doorman or the receptionist had been riling the others up, proposing some kind of mutiny, a strike, maybe, believe it or not, or something else along those lines.

"Those days are over," Mr. Machi said, "we do things differently, always have, we've always talked these issues through."

"Yes. And gotten rid of the undesirables," Chamorro finished the thought before emptying his glass in one swallow.

Mr. Machi grinned in agreement. Even if it was just Chandon, the champagne wasn't half bad.

No point in opening the good shit, he thought. I don't need to butter up this jerkoff.

"So?" he asked.

"Well, some of the guys are scared, you know. Like Carlos, the cook, the guy who called us, he's worried about his job and his kid's job, but what's really getting him is that some crank has come in and is screwing up the family environment at El Imperio," Chamorro said.

"We'd like to know what's happened so we can advise our guys and win over anyone the agitators might be influencing, you know?" he added around a deep, sonorous belch that made his dewlap wiggle.

Mr. Machi explained: he hated temp workers, he didn't like taking on part-timers to fill holes in the schedule, he liked having his own employees at El Imperio. *His employees*: the phrase was crystal clear. Meaning: if the employees were his, why wouldn't he do what he wanted with them?

"My employees, Chamorro," he repeated.

He knew, Mr. Machi did, that the threat of unemployment now did the same job guys like Almirón and Romero used to do for him before: God bless the market economy and the law of supply and demand. There were hardly ever any surprises. Everything worked better and got cheaper all the time. So times were twice as good.

And there was an added benefit, the private and unconfessable pleasure of breaking other people's will. But he didn't say that.

He just spelled it out: *My employees.*

"I never take a day off," he said, gesturing to one of the waiters to bring another bottle of champagne. "And I'm the owner. So if I'm here every day because the business needs me, why should these guys get to call in when the business needs them?"

He paused to see if Chamorro agreed or if he was going to pass judgment in his capacity as a representative of the workers' interests. There it was: he agreed.

"Plus, Pablo knew how things go here," Machi clarified. "I come here to work, they come here to work—am I right or am I right?" he asked, just as the waiter topped off their glasses with more Chandon.

They were both working, Mr. Machi and the waiter, each in his own way, of course.

"Of course, of course, no doubt whatsoever," Chamorro said after thanking Mr. Machi for the wine and singing its praises.

And he proposed a division of labor: they'd take care of the other guys who were stirring up shit, Mr. Machi would take care of the doorman.

"Absolutely," Mr. Machi agreed, "we can even get started now."

"Gustavo!" Mr. Machi called. "Fill up our friend

Chamorro's glass here and send me the door guy and Carlos."

"Sir," the two men summoned said, almost in unison, a few minutes later.

"You," Mr. Machi said to the first, "you're fired, go get changed and come back next week for your check."

"And you, you get a raise, now go back to the kitchen," he said to the second.

"As you wish," said the first, and left.

The other, the cook, Carlos Amante, barely managed to say "Thank you so much, sir, again, thank you," smiling at Chamorro, who tried to hide his astonishment.

"Be sure our friend here is well taken care of," Mr. Machi said to Gustavo.

And then, turning to Chamorro: "Now, if you'll excuse me, I have a lot on my plate . . ."

"Of course, of course," Chamorro answered, and reached out his hand. Mr. Machi pretended not to see it and walked to his office. He listened with displeasure as Chamorro—seated at the very table Mr. Machi kept reserved for congressmen and ambassadors, big-league athletes and ministers, people he plied with liquor, food, and girls brought in by Mariela Báez—Chamorro, the no-name head of the restaurant workers' union, a mere go-between, ordered another bottle "of that wine with the bubbles and a couple of sandwiches on white bread."

"You, follow me," Mr. Machi said to one of the hostesses.

"Yes, sir," she said. The way all of them did.

Now, thirty years later, Mr. Machi could say yes, he liked that power.

PART X

INNUMERABLE

32

HE FEELS RELIEVED. Mr. Machi does. He holds the steering wheel in place with his legs while opening the bottle of Coca-Cola he bought at the Chinese family's mini-mart and taking a sip. The flavor is sweet and sticky and the soda is hot, but his throat is burning with thirst and he drinks it down like cool, clear water. He takes another sip and the bubbles in the syrupy, hot, viscous liquid make him belch. Mr. Machi screws the bottle shut, drops it, emits a thunderous burp, and feels more relieved still. A kind of tranquility suffuses him, and for the first time since he felt the BMW jerk from the blown tire, he breathes calmly and smiles without fear.

He looks in the pocket of his Armani shirt, filthy with blood and soil and vomit and bits of dead body, and digs out the pen. The *S* and the *K* are almost smudged out, but with a little effort, you can read the words SKYLIGHT TANGO BAR.

As he leaves behind the abandoned shack, the overgrown meadow, the screeching, busted, rusty gate, as the

BMW races on like a black bolt of lightning provoking looks of astonishment and envy in its wake, Mr. Machi leaves behind his fear as well, his vertigo, the sense that the world is ending. He throws the pen out the window and watches in the rearview as a truck rolls over it, scattering it in dozens of pieces. It seems inconceivable that it frightened him so as he sees it transformed in the rearview mirror into a cloud of shards that look like flies from afar. Lunatic flies. Annoying, maybe, but they can't scare anyone.

Mr. Machi has a good laugh. He turns on the radio. A Cacho Castaña song comes through the speakers, growling that when all is said and done, life goes on.

33

NOW FOR THE CLOTHES, Mr. Machi thinks, with a serenity extraordinary for this very strange day. He can't believe all that's happened. And in so little time.

How long ago was it that the chick with the blond mane was kneeling between his legs? With a little effort, he can still feel her lips tighten on his dick, still taste the tobacco, the pristine cocaine. He checks his Rolex to see if it's really true that his life fell to pieces that fast. And that he needed so little time to put it back together. He's tired, he figures he must look like hell, but something resembling happiness invades him.

I just need a shower to feel like myself again, he thinks.

A line, he thinks, a smoke.

He thinks: some clean clothes. A black Brioni suit, one of the red Marinella ties from his collection. The clean clothes Mr. Machi thinks of are exclusive, like everything else he owns. Exclusive, costly.

"Instruments for the ratification of a reality that may

only be obtained by means of said objects," Alejandro Wilkinson used to say.

If it's tobacco, it's Cohiba, or else Montecristo. If it's a lighter, it's a Dupont. The watch is a Rolex; the pen, a Montblanc; the shoes, Crockett & Jones; suits and shirts are Brioni, Armani, Versace, or Scappino. Ties: Italian silk, preferably Marinella. Whiskey, Chivas. Car, BMW, of course, or a Mercedes or even an Audi. Someday it'll be a Rolls or a Bentley, he thinks.

"That's new-money swagger," his father-in-law, Mirta's old man, still says with contempt.

Sure, Mr. Machi always thinks, easy for you to say: son, grandson, great-grandson of a dynasty, born in the lap of luxury, owner of half of Santa Fe.

"Objects reaffirm the individual and also his social context," Alejandro Wilkinson used to repeat.

"They're showy, vulgar, and they've got no class, those new-money types like your friend," Mirta's father used to preach to her. "They don't buy things, they buy symbols, and they think that if they do so, they can buy their way into having real class."

"You need to learn how to live, my boy, now that you're part of the family," the old man told him those first few times.

Mr. Machi swallowed and gritted his teeth.

New money, he thought. It wasn't the words that got to him so much as the condescension in the old man's tone.

"Self-made man, Machi," Alejandro Wilkinson used to

tell him, "keep repeating that phrase. That's what we are: self-made men."

New money means guys who did it their way, Mr. Machi tells himself. That very night, he's going to dress to the nines, he thinks. The Brioni suit he bought last winter in Naples, the lavender blue Versace shirt, and the red silk tie Thaelman gave him for New Year's.

"But first you gotta deal with *this*, Luisito," he says to his face in the rearview. Sure, it looks like hell, but there's a glimmer of something in it that resembles happiness.

He makes a mental list.

Once he gets home and changes clothes, he needs to work things out with Mirta.

Mirta, the ball-breaker, he thinks to himself.

I'm going to have to promise her something, he reckons, a round-the-world cruise, a yacht, something big.

Next thing is to call Cesspit, he thinks—his confidence in his security chief suddenly restored—and have him find out how they could get hold of my BMW or else dump the body inside it. And then take care of whoever's responsible.

We can't have things like this happening.

If Cesspit had wanted to fuck me, it would have been me showing up in someone else's trunk, and not the other way around, he thinks. And the guy's not gonna bite the hand that feeds him. I'm all he's got. How could I have suspected him, he asks, how could I have doubted.

But the doubt doesn't go away. Once a doubt creeps in, it's not easy to dislodge it.

These next few weeks, Mr. Machi decides, the best thing will be to find someone to take care of Cesspit, who's scraped together a lot of power in those bloodstained hands of his.

He opens back up the bottle of Coke and takes another warm sip.

Too much power, he thinks.

34

THREE EXITS BEFORE the one that will take him home, he makes a final stop. He pulls up to a rickety kiosk, a shack with a single window. A girl waits on him, no older than eleven. A brat with long, slender arms. She's got crust in her eyes, ashy, unwashed hair, and a flowery dress draped over a body showing the tiny beginnings of breasts. The girl gets on tiptoe to reach the counter behind the window of the makeshift kiosk.

"What can I get for you, sir?" she asks.

"A box of matches and a peanut bar," Mr. Machi responds.

"Big or small?" the brat asks, squinting her crusty eyes in what looks like a naughty or maybe a mocking smile.

"The peanut bar or the matches?" Mr. Machi asks her back.

The brat looks at him cheekily, almost like they were equals. Now there's no mistaking the mockery in her smile.

"Whichever you prefer, sir," she says. "I'm here to serve."

"Big for the peanut bar, small for the matches," Mr. Machi barks, slightly irritated.

Little cunt, he thinks.

Rude little cunt.

"Oh, okay," the girl says, and stretches to look up at the shelf over the window. She steps on a case of soda to reach it. For an instant, the window frames her small breasts in her flowery dress while the girl reaches up and feels around. Then she steps down, sets the matches and the peanut bar on the counter, and asks if Mr. Machi needs anything else.

Though he doesn't know why, really, all of a sudden, she reminds him of Luciana. She doesn't look like Luciana, and she's filthy, but something about the girl's sass reminds him of his own daughter when she was ten, maybe eleven years old. Those nascent breasts are just the first step, he thinks. A few years from now she'll fuck off and move in with some douchebag with a beard. Just like Luciana. He's indignant as he recalls his daughter, her embarrassment of a boyfriend, her insistence on pursuing a stupid and pointless major. He remembers that she's supposed to drop by tonight to pick up that piece of shit book that hundreds of Dunas, Peugeot 504s, and Renault 19s must have run over by now. He thinks of other things, too; he couldn't even count all the things that he thinks of in that moment.

"Anything else?" the brat asks again, scrubbing the crust from her eyes.

Mr. Machi wants to get under her skin, to offend her a little bit. Creep her out. Scare her. Something. His voice stiffens, same as his features.

"A box of rubbers," he says.

"Which ones?" the girl asks, smiling again. "We've got lubricated, studded, extra thin—"

"Any of 'em, babe, just give me a pack," Mr. Machi interrupts her, again seeing Luciana at ten, eleven years old. Then he grabs everything, pays, and stalks off without waiting for his change.

He walks back to the BMW, takes the bottle of lighter fluid out of one of the Chinese mini-mart bags, puts the dead man's clothes inside, and sets off on foot. He leaves behind the kiosk, the BMW, his daughter's memory, the avenue, and looks around. Three blocks up, he finds what he's looking for. The corner is deserted, there's no lid on the trash can. He puts the bag of clothes inside and sprays it down with lighter fluid until the bottle is empty. Then he throws the bottle in, too. He lights a match and looks at the flame for an instant before dropping it inside. He makes sure it catches, then drops the rest of the box over the top of his miniature bonfire. When the flames start to climb, he turns around and walks back to the BMW with long strides, eating his peanut bar along the way, while behind him, farther and farther off, the trash can burns, burns, burns.

And burns.

PART XI

DRAWN

WITH A

FINE BRUSH

MADE WITH

CAMEL HAIR

35

HE WAS LOVED BY HIS COWORKERS,
Pablo was. Maybe that's why Mr. Machi
thought, for a moment, that someone
would do something.

But no.

He called together all the workers at El Imperio to tell
them the news himself: the new system, the way things
would work from then on out. He usually sent someone
else, Eduardo or one of the office girls, but not this time.
With the affection they felt for Pablo and with the 2001
protests against the banks and the government and that
little bullshit slogan "Throw them all out," he didn't need
people stepping out of line.

"So on your off days, an hour before your normal start
time, call in and check to see if we need you, understood?"
Mr. Machi said, more as an affirmation than a question.

"Don't wait for us to call you, call and ask yourself," he
added, as if there were any need to.

He looked at the thirty or so men and women sitting
in front of him in silence, trying to hide their displeasure,

most staring at the floor, looking for some hole to crawl into.

"I don't want any more problems like we had yesterday," he said.

"Now, everyone get to work," he said.

No one so much as uttered Pablo's name. Mr. Machi was satisfied. And calm. Rabble-rousers, he thought, that's it for the rabble-rousers.

Pablo had worked as a waiter for all thirty years of his adult life. He knew the secrets of the service profession better than anyone, from the most formal (the placement of the cutlery, how to write out the orders, which side of the customer to serve from) to the most ineffable (when to be seen and when to vanish, which customers needed the luxury treatment and which ones wanted you to act like their friend). For eighteen of those thirty years, he'd worked under Mr. Machi's command. Pablo knew the rules after all that time: discretion, obedience, readiness to work, and obedience again for good measure. He knew them, and he followed them. That's why he'd made it through the meat grinder of the past few years. That's why.

After all, you made good money at El Imperio. Despite the miserable wages. Despite the fact that part of those miserable wages were paid under the table. Even despite having to grease Eduardo's palm to get the good tables. Yes, despite all that—between El Imperio's reputation; the grade-A shows; the strength of the dollar, which made Buenos Aires a cheap city for mobs of tourists; and his natural aptitude for the waiter's vocation—he left El Imperio each night with his pockets bursting with tips. Pablo lived alone, and had for more than a decade. His kids were grown and his wife had left him a long time back, tired of the cold, lonely nights. Since then, Pablo lived in a small pension on the Calle Bolivar.

"This is a cuckold's business," he used to mumble. "When the time comes to heat things up between the sheets, we're always working. So you gotta take the backdoor-man factor as a given," and he would laugh a joyless, spiritless laugh.

Every night—along with Pipa, Muqueño, and one or two of the guys—he'd go to a club on the Calle Moreno, around the corner from the police station, to eat fries, play cards, and knock back a few beers until he got so tired it wasn't so dispiriting going back to the pension.

But there was something else. A brown-skinned little doll. A girl from Tucumán with dark eyes, killer curves, and a naughty smile that drove Pablo wild. She shook her hips, this girl from Tucumán, her white teeth glimmering in her face as she pranced between the tables serving empanadas. She could sing, too. If someone stepped up with a guitar and the food and drinks were on the tables, she'd belt out "La Pomeña" or "Doña Ubenza." And every time this happened, Pablo would think about asking her out, taking her to the movies or something like that. He had waking dreams about those curves under the soft yellow light of his room.

"How am I gonna do that with this job, though," he complained to Pipa and Muqueño the night before the decisive one. "It's gotta be on a Monday."

"A Monday when we don't have a double billing," Muqueño threw out from behind his glass of cold beer.

"Enough with your moaning, mister. You sound like a faggot," said Pipa, who liked to call everyone mister or miss, no matter how close they were. "What more could you ask for than a chick who serves tables and keeps the same hours as you? That reduces the absence factor and the backdoor-man factor along with it. Invite her to spend the day in Tigre or something next time we just have one act on a Monday."

"But she works Mondays." Pablo went back to whining, self-indulgent and timorous, but also excited.

Let me explain something.

The evening before their only day off each week—which always fell sometime between Monday and Thursday— every employee at El Imperio, but particularly the waiters, had to check the schedule before leaving to see if a double act was booked for the next night. If a double act was booked, it went without saying they had to give up their day off. Mr. Machi didn't like people trading shifts. He'd pay you, but you had to come in. And there were times when this happened every week for months on end.

So Pablo waited and waited. He waited one week, then the next, scared stiff that someone might jump the line and the girl would be taken by the time he got his chance to ask her out. He waited, watching her smile with her ivory-white teeth, serving fried empanadas and wiggling her hips between the tables. He waited, playing endless card games and hearing her croon "Cantora de Yala" amid shouts of "raise" and "hold."

Until finally, with the first heat of September, when the blossoms on the trees in the Plaza de Mayo covered the sky with violet, a Sunday came when Eduardo told him there was only one show planned for tomorrow, and he could finally take his day off.

"For now," he added, loosening a black-and-yellow tie he considered the height of good taste. "If anything changes, we'll call you tomorrow."

"Or else," Pablo tried, knowing that trying was futile, "you could call in Gustavo. He hasn't gotten any overtime in a while."

"You know Machi doesn't like people switching out," was Eduardo's predictable reply.

"Yeah, but . . ."

"I'll set you up with the good tables if you have to come in. Don't sweat it, I'll make it worth your while," Eduardo said with a wink. He was trying to buddy up to him, but all Pablo could think of was the girl.

"All right then, see you Tuesday."

And he asked her out that very night. It took three beers and a bit of shoving from Pipa before he gathered the courage to do so.

"A day in Tigre," he said, "now that it's getting nice out."

"We could go for a boat ride," he said.

"What do you think," he said.

The girl opened her eyes wide and then batted her eyelashes.

"About time you made up your mind," she said, smiling, and her teeth lit up the whole nightclub—lit Pablo up, too. And since they were heading out early and didn't want to waste any time the next morning—the train to Tigre takes more than an hour—they decided to spend the night together.

The truth is, Pablo was half kidding when he proposed it, because he was tipsy and euphoric, but the girl said of course, what else did he expect, he should wait for her, they'd be closing down soon.

"Your place or mine?" she asked at the door, as the dawn spread out over the Calle Moreno. They chose hers.

Pablo's cell woke them up at two in the afternoon. Pablo stretched, looked in disbelief at the girl's nude convexities, and decided he wouldn't pick up.

"Hey," she said.

"Hey, beautiful, you look so good today," Pablo replied, because it was true, and because he wanted to see her laugh. She laughed. Pablo's phone rang again.

"Why aren't you picking up?" the girl asked, getting out of bed naked to boil water for maté. "You married?"

If I don't look, it's like it's not happening, Pablo thought. If I don't pick up, it's like I never heard it. Doubt gnawed at his conscience like a starving rat. He'd never ignored a call from El Imperio, never missed a shift in eighteen years.

"No! Married. Give me a break," he said. "Must be work."

"You gotta go in?" the girl asked.

Discretion, obedience, readiness to work, and obedience again, Pablo remembered. The meat grinder, he remembered. He thought of all the people he'd seen fired those eighteen years for far less than not showing up on their off day. And he thought of those succulent tips. But just as the teeth of the rodent of doubt were undermining his desire, the girl came to ask once more if he had to go, and Pablo saw her, naked, maté in hand.

"Nah, I'll tell them I lost my phone or something," he said with growing joy—a feeling he'd forgotten over all his years of solitude—throbbing now in his chest.

But it didn't last.

The next day, when he showed up for work, Eduardo didn't let him in the door.

"Machi's orders," he said. "Here's your check, sign for it," he added, and handed him one of the last pens left over from the days of the Skylight.

"What happened yesterday?" he asked, as if he even

cared, just to make Pablo realize what a small thing he'd lost his job over.

"I couldn't find my phone, Eduardo, and anyway, it was my day off, I was in Tigre, I mean," Pablo blubbered, "they're not gonna let me go after all these years just for that!"

Eduardo cut him off.

"You know how Machi is."

"But," Pablo said, and then he didn't say anything more. He thought of how hard everything would be now without a job. Of the money he had to give his daughters, of the pension. He thought of the girl: she was a little old to be babysitting some jobless prick.

"Anyway . . . you knew we might need you," Eduardo finished with the one thought his tiny brain managed to formulate.

"Tell Machi he'll pay for this," Pablo said, handing him back the pen.

"Keep it, as a souvenir," Eduardo said with a scornful, condescending smile tugging at the corners of his lips.

"He'll pay," Pablo repeated. "You tell him."

36 FOR THREE LONG YEARS, he'd managed to avoid meeting him. In part because Luciana hadn't brought the guy around much, in part because this Federico or Felipe—he never figured out which—didn't seem too interested in showing his face or getting to know the rest of the family, and finally because, on the few occasions when the boyfriend did come around, Mr. Machi cut out under the pretext of work or some unforeseen business trip.

He wasn't keen on having to stare at the bearded face—the beard looks nice on him, Luciana always said—of this Felipe or Federico that was knocking his daughter's boots.

But this time, there was no getting around it. Luciana had come to them saying she wanted to move in with her boyfriend and they'd managed to get an apartment. They were moving on Thursday, and she invited the three of them—Mr. Machi, Mirta, and Alan—to come to lunch the following Saturday.

"Me and Fe thought we'd do it early in the day so Papi

could come, too," she said. And that left Mr. Machi without an escape hatch.

The kid—this Federico or Felipe—had a couple of years on Luciana, but he didn't have a degree. He wasn't studying, either. He worked odd jobs.

"He just does whatever comes along," Luciana repeated proudly. "He's a writer."

So this Felipe or Federico did whatever job came along to keep himself afloat as a writer. Mr. Machi could imagine this bearded shit-for-brains sticking it inside his daughter and thinking about her father's millions and how, with them, he could go on writing without a care.

Probably writes poems, Mr. Machi thought.

"So what does he write?" he asked.

"Stories, mostly," Luciana gushed. "He's finishing a novel now, a detective novel."

The apartment was in Congreso; it was a matchbox full of books and black-and-white photos of people who were presumably dead. Mr. Machi wrinkled his nose.

"How's it going," Federico or Felipe said, reaching out his hand, after greeting Mirta and Alan with a kiss on the cheek.

"Who's that one," was Mr. Machi's only response, as he pointed out a photo at random.

"Dashiell Hammett, an American who—"

"I don't like Americans," Mr. Machi cut him short, considering the conversation finished. "I prefer the English, the English are the ones who invented everything."

And that more or less set the tone for the rest of their lunch.

"Don't you drink wine?" asked Felipe. Or Federico.

"Yeah, but good wine . . . Why didn't you say you needed some, Luciana? I would have brought a bottle."

"Luis, please," Mirta jumped in. "Since when do we—?"

"Since I've been able to pay for it," Mr. Machi snapped, ill-humored.

"Papa," Luciana cut in. "Don't be nasty."

And she gave him a loving shove, defusing the situation. Then she kissed her boyfriend—that grimy beard is touching my daughter's mouth! Mr. Machi thought—and told him not to pay Papa any mind, he was always like that at first.

"He's a brute," Alan said, seconding his sister. "You'll have to forgive him."

The kid, Federico or Felipe, didn't respond right away. No, he thought, he wouldn't forgive him, and yes, he would pay him mind. Just then, he decided he would write a novel with Mr. Machi as protagonist, and terrible things would happen to him. He poured himself a glass of wine and drank it in the lingering silence, not looking at anyone.

"No problem," he said, finally.

37

"POUR ME A WHISKEY, will you, my throat's dry as a bone.

"What do you mean, high? Fuming is what I am. Asshole thinks he can lecture me. Your old man was born with a silver spoon in his mouth so he thinks that gives him the right to get all preachy!

"You know what it would take to get rid of your old man? One phone call, that's it. Don't make faces at me—one phone call, I promise you. His day is done, Mirta, and he can't seem to get that through his head. His name doesn't scare anyone anymore, got it?

"I built an empire, babe, that's no bullshit. I started with nothing. Work ethic, my pops used to say—God bless his soul—and you know what, he didn't understand either, the old bastard.

"It seems easy now, it looks like a cakewalk, but someone had to make it happen, okay? I had to keep my eyes peeled, make the right moves. Like your blowhard of a father could have done it—like he could have figured out the score.

"A tumbledown factory, that's all I had! Not acres and acres of farmland and cattle and a fancy last name. No. Just a textile factory! And the bar we set up with a couple of friends. That's it. But I saw. I saw what was coming, because I'm a businessman, a self-made man, like Alejandro.

"Like your old man could have ever pulled that off!

"It's easy to talk when you've been loaded for three generations, but you've got to know how to fight for your money, make every peso count, study what works and what doesn't. Like the pens from the Skylight: I ran the numbers and I bought them when the dollar was down, and later, when things went to shit and Buenos Aires filled up with tourists, I sold them as souvenirs at the end of our shows, and we made out like bandits. That's why I held on to a few, for the memories, and I still use them to sign important documents, understand? That's how much of a profit we made. And back then, too, when the shows, the club, everything was on the skids.

"So I'm high, huh? So what—I don't see you paying for the shit. I don't see your old man buying it for me. I don't see anyone donating it to me, thanks to your fancy last name. Pour me a whiskey, will you, and listen to what I'm trying to tell you. Pay attention!

"I was saying that even though the Skylight wasn't El Imperio and everything was in the toilet, we still made money regardless. Why? Well, you tell me. Because I took advantage of opportunities, that's why. Because I was sharp and it's better to be slick than be smart. See if you can get that into your head . . .

"Sure, the shows were pure sleaze. The food? Mediocre or worse. Say what you want, but I took advantage of every chance that came along, okay? And I followed Alejandro's advice—your old man always hated him because he was a self-made man and not the son and grandson and great-grandson of some fat cat like him—and I made the right friends and they kept me up on which way the wind was blowing. And then I did what I had to do. Things your old man didn't have the guts for, or the cunning, despite his fancy last name. Things my old man would have called immoral, or some shit.

"I got my hands dirty, sure. I got dirty all the way to my eyebrows! And now you people want to come preach to me?

"And I won't have your dear old dad telling me how I ought to live. Same way I didn't let my old man tell me. That hard-nosed dago couldn't see anything but work and more work, no time for friends, no time to enjoy his money. But that's not how you do business or hit the big time! That's how you get a heart attack. Work, that's for niggers!

"Could you people have seen the potential in the XL Group, the benefits of merging with Varano and liquidating Machitex? And if we hadn't done that, how would we have made it to the big leagues with El Imperio, tell me that? You think you all would have had the foresight? Tell me . . . Or tell your old man to tell me, since he thinks he knows so much.

"No: our fathers wouldn't have seen what was coming. They're too shortsighted, the both of them. You had to listen to the whispers in the hallways, on the street, where the real power is, get it, Mirta?

"Look at this pen: this is what you make cash with, this. Signing papers at just the right time.

"I'm going to the bathroom, I'll be right back. Make me another whiskey, will you . . .

"Where's that whiskey I asked for?

"About time. Go ahead and pour me another while you're at it.

"Take the factory, for example. You wanna know where the fuck we were headed with that shithole when the dollar was on par with the peso? Straight down the toilet, that's where! My old man? I'll tell you what he would have done: put his shoulder to the wheel and worked, worked, worked. Yours wouldn't have even done that! All he does is ride his horses, count his cows, and talk with that tight-assed accent of his about your ancestors and God knows what else. But words won't do it: you gotta think fast and be merciless and act. Like when we had to set fire to the Skylight to collect the insurance.

"Don't bust my balls, Mirta. Where the fuck are my whiskeys? And look, if the mood strikes me and I want another rail, I'll do it right here and now and you'll watch me and enjoy it. Look, I'll snort it through one of my magnificent Skylight pens, okay? One of these collector's items I bought for chump change and sold for hard cash.

"With one of these! These are what you do business with!

"Look. I did what I had to do.

"I passed the factory over to the investors at Varano, we issued bonds, we stripped the motherfucker down, and we declared bankruptcy a few years later. In '92 all we had was a second-rate textile plant and in '94 I could put two million just into remodeling the club, see? And then we brought on Old Man Lazzaro and the rest of the heavy hitters for the orchestra and we started to play in the big leagues.

"I turned El Imperio into an empire!

"Despite my old man bellyaching about the factory and yours coming to offer me life lessons. I don't know why I bother telling you all this, you're even more clueless than they are.

"I'm still waiting for my goddamn whiskey."

PART XII

ET CETERA

38 SOON, SOON. I'll be leaving this nightmare behind me, Mr. Machi thinks, again behind the wheel of his black two-hundred-thousand-dollar bolt of lightning, which cuts across the filthy asphalt, leaving looks of astonishment and envy in its wake.

He pulls over on the side of the highway, takes out the Whave chain cutter, and in one clink gets the handcuffs off the hinge in his trunk. He throws them out to the middle of the road and stands there watching them get flattened, a stupid smug smile on his lips. Just as with with the pen from the Skylight, he is enjoying the sight of the fur handcuffs, which so terrified him just a few hours before—or was it less? or much more? Mr. Machi has lost track of time, and no white gold Rolex in the world could orient him now—being transformed into an inoffensive, amorphous, grayish mass beneath the wheels of cars and trucks.

Soon, soon, he reminds himself, still standing immobile, while the Dunas, the Peugeot 504s, and the Renault 19s do their work.

Then, behind him, in the BMW's passenger seat, his cell phone rings. Mr. Machi gets in and looks at it, unnerved, as if a prehistoric animal, long extinct, has just climbed into his car. He lets it ring twice before he picks up.

"Machi," he says.

"Did we say you were going to call me today?" he asks. "At this hour?"

"Okay," he says, "I'll be there in fifteen."

He says, "Yeah, bag me up twenty grams."

"But go by the club tonight for your payment," he says. "I'm out of cash."

The BMW takes off, swift as a bolt of lightning, and again turns off its intended route on this morning that seems to never end.

39 A LITTLE WHILE LATER, Mr. Machi drives on, a few lines warming his nose and cooling his thoughts. He starts unraveling his list of suspects.

Briefly, he laughs at his initial apprehensions.

The girls, for example. How was Colorada or the other one going to cook up a plot like this?

And Gladis? Even less likely.

He admits he would have liked to fuck the Paraguayan a few more times. Mr. Machi licks his lips and all at once it seems to him that the clouds crossing the azure sky have the shape of thick thighs and bouncy breasts.

Or Alan's little boyfriend, he thinks. For God's sake, like that faggot was ever going to pose some kind of threat!

Boyfriend, *faggot*, the words resound in Mr. Machi's head, producing a deafening echo.

I gotta do something about that kid, he thinks, and shakes his head the way he always does when the vision of Alan hugging that slender blond with the lagging gait comes into his mind.

It couldn't have been him, either. Of course not.

There had been a concatenation of coincidences, no doubt about it. His cell, for example. It's working fine now. Scared the hell out of him before, and now it's working fine.

Speaking of, he thinks.

Not stopping the car, he calls Cesspit.

"I need you at El Imperio this afternoon around six-ish, there's a thing we gotta talk about," he says as soon as his bloodhound responds.

"What happened today that you didn't pick up when I called?" he asks.

And without giving Cesspit time to answer, he adds: "You can explain it to me this afternoon."

Then he hangs up.

He drops the phone in the passenger seat and returns to the list.

The more Mr. Machi thinks about it, the clearer it is that he was never the target, that there was some kind of security lapse at El Imperio that someone took advantage of, and his car being involved was pure chance: right place, wrong time. Whatever was at the root of it, it wasn't about him; it was about that thing he left lying in the meadow by an abandoned shack on the outskirts of Moreno.

Patrón Casal, he thinks.

No, he wouldn't get his hands dirty over that whore of a wife. These soccer types know they're asking for it with their pregame meetings and all that time on the road. One way or another, it's a risk they're willing to take.

Besides, how many times did that asshole leave El Imperio with one or two of Mariela Báez's girls on his arm?

Mirta—but what would she have to gain from something like this? Not cash, anyway. Spoiled brats like her never give money a second thought.

"The only way not to think about money is to have it," as Alejandro Wilkinson used to say.

To have it as long as you've lived, for as long as you're going to live. Not so much money itself as the security money brings.

Anyway, Mr. Machi knows Mirta loves him. She's a ball-breaker, sure, but she loves him. She wouldn't do anything to hurt him.

On one side of the road is a stand selling knockoff sportswear. The kind of clothes his waiters must buy, or Gladis must buy for her kid. Adibas tracksuits, Mike shoes, Reebot T-shirts.

Mr. Machi stops the BMW alongside the vendor, cracks the window, and buys, with what's left in his wallet, a pair of sneakers, size ten, a polo, and a combo windbreaker and track pants.

A few miles farther on, he stops on the shoulder and changes in the car without cutting the motor.

About time to get rid of that blood, vomit, and dirt, Mr. Machi thinks.

Then he curses a few times under his breath. This shit is getting expensive: besides the bribe for the two cops (and the Glock, which was a memento of Loco Wilkinson, damn it), besides the hacksaw and the Whave chain cutter, besides the time wasted and the irritation, he's lost a fine-looking Scappino and a three-hundred-dollar Armani shirt. But there's no way around it, once blood dries, you can't get it out, as Mr. Machi knows from his days in the textile biz. The tie, luckily, is salvageable: an Italian silk number from his collection of almost three hundred. The rest of Machi's threads get wadded into a ball and tossed into the sportswear bag.

Now, in his blue Adibas tracksuit, Mr. Machi thinks again about Old Man Heredia.

Another birdbrained idea, he thinks. The old man wouldn't have the means.

Mr. Machi remembers his snub nose and cauliflower ears from years and years of punches and the friction of stiff laces from fourteen- or sixteen-ounce gloves; brown gloves on hard, grainy hands. He remembers his beer belly and the few teeth the sport hadn't robbed him of, how they glowed such a pure white. He remembers the old man's deep voice, the deliberate, indifferent way he used to talk when anything but boxing was the subject. Finally, he remembers his heartbreak when Martínez died. An enormous, consummate, perfect chagrin. A sorrow like losing a son, a last chance, a departing train.

Something in Heredia's life ended forever when Martínez killed himself. Mr. Machi knew that.

Still and all, it was ludicrous to suspect the old man, he thinks, not even bothering to finish the thought.

Anyway, he adds in automatic self-justification, it was just a little fixed fight, nothing out of the ordinary.

They can't hang it on him, he thinks. Martínez was the one who decided to put a bullet in his dome. Every time you turn around, some boxer's going to the pen or else getting his brains beat out. Is he gonna have to take the blame every time one of those lowlifes kicks the bucket?

Madness.

And with the notable absence of anonymous corpses in the trunk of his car, Mr. Machi feels a forgotten enthusiasm and joy springing up in the place where fear has lately dwelt. And he's reasoning more clearly.

Philosophically, he thinks: it's incredible what fear can do to your mind.

Incredible.

Pablo, for example—how could he ever have accused him? The poor bastard, all he knows how to do is serve food without fucking it up. Mr. Machi grins when he thinks how Pipa's now the one plowing that chick from Tucumán that Pablo lost his job over. Then he wonders who told him that and since when does he listen to gossip about his workers. Who the fuck cares. Mr. Machi smiles again, and that smile gives way to unforced laughter. He's laughing out loud now. Hard. Cackling. Aside from seeing some old bag trip and fall down in the street, nothing tickles Mr. Machi more than when one guy steals another guy's broad. Especially when the first guy was dumb enough to lose his job over said broad.

Behind the wheel, he feels his pulse steady, his breathing calm, his vision clear.

Incredible, the shit I had myself believing, he thinks, now that he's feeling relieved.

The commies from the factory, for example—how long ago was all that? Thirty, thirty-two years?

"Give me a break!" he says indignantly, as if scolding a child.

You know damn good and well they rubbed those fuckers out, Romero and Almirón weren't the type to forgive. And who's going to cook up this kind of complicated scheme to avenge them thirty-some years later? Not even the Reds are that vindictive. Besides, Cesspit can smell them from a mile off: he knows how they walk, how they move their hands, their tone of voice.

Madness, he repeats, at the very moment when a green sign rises up in his field of vision, announcing the exit he needs to take to reach his next destination, the last before he returns home.

He turns without slowing down.

That's why I drive a two-hundred-thousand-dollar machine, he thinks.

40

LAST STOP. Mr. Machi thinks, not knowing if this is true or just an expression of desire as he parks at the shopping center, where he seems to remember there's a branch of a chain bookstore. The only book and CD store in the area. He tries to remember if they know him, if he's ever set foot inside the place. He doesn't think so.

He doesn't like bookstores, and he only goes to shopping centers on trips to Miami: Aventura, Sawgrass, Zambrano's, those are malls. Malls, he thinks, like the Yankees call them. Sears, Marshalls, JCPenney, those are real stores.

He's certain he's never been to this place before.

Better that way, he thinks.

He feels a little ridiculous wearing his Adibas tracksuit with Versace glasses, so he slips them into one of the pockets. He wonders if anyone will notice his bootleg clothes, but more or less at the same time, he decides it doesn't matter. He knows perfectly well what he's there for.

"You take cards, right?" he asks the counter girl, a

blond in her twenties, who answers indifferently, not looking up from her magazine, "Yes: Mastercard, Amex, and Visa, minimum purchase seventy pesos."

Mr. Machi sees her as a chance to confirm that he's made it through this shit, that he's back to being himself. He taps the counter three times with his index finger and uses a tone he finds pleasing, one he recognizes himself in.

"I'm talking to you, sweet cheeks," he says.

"Yes?" the girl responds, marking her page in the magazine, leaving it open with front and back covers facing up—*Is it true that Mariano Trossini left his wife because he was cheating on her with another dancer from his show?*—like a butterfly of ass-kissing celebrity worship about to rise up and take flight.

"Credit cards, you take them?"

"Yes, I just told you. Mastercard, Amex, and Visa, minimum purchase seventy pesos."

"Right," Mr. Machi says, his tone growing more and more commanding, "but what you didn't say was *sir*, and you didn't ask me what I need. Can we start there?" He's sure he's hit the mark, that he's on the right road, back in his habitual role. And that this counter girl should have understood what that role was from the start.

"Yes, sir, please accept my apologies," the girl agrees, placing her magazine under the counter. As if she understands all of a sudden that it's unthinkable to read while attending to a customer of this kind.

"What are you looking for? How can I help you?"

And she repeats: "Sir."

He smiles, pleased, Mr. Machi does, contented. He realizes he's standing tall again and that he's master of the situation. He coughs two or three times, just to hear his own cough, just to make the girl wait. Then he savors her attitude, sedulous and servile. It takes her a while to understand which book he's looking for, with the confused and fragmentary information he can give her.

Ten minutes later, she finds it, and asks if he needs anything else, hoping the response will be no.

"Yeah, give me another book that might interest Luciana," Mr. Machi replies. And waits.

The counter girl hesitates. How can she know what kind of books this guy's daughter likes?

"By the same author?" she ventures, embarrassed to find she doesn't even know how to pronounce the name.

Seeing her embarrassment, Mr. Machi grows larger still, girds himself, and the words flow out as though dictated by his own personal demiurge.

"For ten minutes I've been telling you what Luciana reads, doll, now give me another book that might interest her."

"Of course, sir." The counter girl excuses herself, and calls a psychologist friend and collates results from a web search with the stock at the bookstore.

And so, along with *The Order of Things*, Mr. Machi

takes *Writing Degree Zero* by Barthes and two Sidney Sheldon novels for Mirta. He also buys a DVD of a show from Madonna's most recent tour for Alan, and two CDs for himself: one by Ricardo Arjona and one by Diego Torres.

"Gift wrap it," he says, "and I want each item in its own bag."

He exits the store while the young blond counter girl's various sirs—yes, sir; of course, sir; anything else I can help you with, sir; we hope to see you again soon, sir—soothe his ears like a lingering caress.

41

BEFORE GOING BACK to the BMW, Mr. Machi stops in at the restroom to powder his nose.

Now, yes.

Sitting in the bucket seat he himself chose the leather for, which feels like a young girl's ass, he tears open the packages of books and CDs and uses the wrappings for the Scappino suit and the Armani shirt ruined by bloodstains, vomit, and dirt, and stuffs them both back in the bag the tracksuit, polo shirt, and sneakers came in. He stuffs the six bags from the bookstore in on top, dumps inside the lukewarm, leftover Coke, puts the plastic bottle inside, too, and ties the whole package in a knot.

He gets out of the BMW, walks unhurriedly, and looks.

A few blocks away, he finds some dogshit still loose enough to serve his purposes. He smiles with an almost childish mischief before smearing the bag. Then he wrinkles his nose, hurries over to the nearest tree, and drops the bag beside it.

The sun is shining up high, and its light is of a filthy

splendor vaguely reminiscent of marble, of melted butter, of bone, or of wool on the body of a dying sheep.

"No one's gonna go snooping in that filth," Mr. Machi thinks, and slips back on his sunglasses.

It's close to being over, he thinks.

PART XIII

THAT

JUST

BROKE

THE JUG

42

THE ENTRANCE TO the subdivision where the Machi family resides looks like an enormous golf course dotted with the odd mansion. The perimeter, hedged by high green privet trimmed meticulously by an army of gardeners twice a week, has a guard shack every twelve yards. They spend, they spend big, the residents of El Barrio—they like calling it that, *El Barrio*, it gives them a feeling of simplicity, of sincerity, a countrified touch, as if this were paradise regained—on watchmen, cameras, alarms . . . on the fiction of security.

"You just can't live in Buenos Aires anymore," the neighbors in El Barrio often say to their friends who still reside in presumptuous urban palaces in neighborhoods like Las Cañitas or Barrio Parque. "When you least expect it, some son of a bitch could put a bullet in your head at a stoplight."

"Plus," the women usually add, "the kids have got their friends here, they're growing up in contact with nature," and then they point at their frolicking children.

They frolic, the children of those parents who can't live in Buenos Aires anymore for fear that some son of a bitch, some black son of a bitch, will blow out their brains at a stoplight. They frolic on lawns meticulously mowed every three days by an army of gardeners. They frolic with other kids, identical to them, the little friends their parents handpick. They frolic, watched over by strategically placed cameras.

Security cameras, lookouts, armed guards, swimming pools, and hundreds of gardeners manicuring the grass: the return to nature in El Barrio.

Due west of the privet hedge is the gate, two automatic doors with three security guards watching over them.

Mr. Machi hits the button for the gate and nods in greeting to the sentry who walks over.

He revs the BMW restlessly.

"Good morning, Señor Luis, Señora Mirta left a message that—" the guard manages to say before Mr. Machi interrupts him, not listening—"later, later"—and speeds off in a way unbecoming of the high-priced tranquility of El Barrio.

Get home, he thinks, just get home.

43

AS SOON AS he enters his house, Mr. Machi feels that his troubles are over, that all that's left of his little problem is a strange, dark anecdote to retell in three or four years' time, one that no one from his inner circle will believe. He laughs off his fears, his suspicions, his worries that his lucky star might have gone dark.

I'm a fortunate guy, he thinks. If I hadn't run over the caltrops, if I hadn't blown a tire, who knows when I'd have figured out that the thing—in his thoughts, it's still just a thing—was back there.

He imagines someone finding it when he took the BMW for a wash, and something of his earlier jitteriness returns. But the anxiety is fleeting. He's in his home, and that thing is in a vacant lot behind an abandoned house in La Reja he couldn't find his way back to even at gunpoint after all that morning's twists and turns.

He returns to being—to feeling—himself. A businessman.

And to believing that businessmen have rivals, competitors, employees, and partners, but not enemies.

Now for a shower, a nice breakfast, and a bit of shut-eye, he thinks.

"Mirta," he shouts, "I'm home."

But he doesn't get an answer.

Did the crazy bitch leave again? he wonders. Doesn't she get bored with these theatrics, playing the betrayed wife running off to cry to her parents?

"Mirta," he repeats.

Mirta doesn't answer.

Just as well, Mr. Machi thinks, and cuts out two lines on the Carrara marble tabletop in the living room.

He snorts once.

Twice.

He lays down two more, just for the hell of it. And snorts.

Then he takes a deep breath, pinches his nostrils, shakes his head a little. He moves his jaw from side to side and purses his lips. He makes a face that is almost a smile.

Then he puts what's left of the cocaine in a porcelain vase on the marble tabletop.

Guillote, he likes to call the thing, in homage to Guillermo Coppola. In the Coppola case, when they busted him with five hundred grams uncut stuffed down inside one, he protested, "That vase isn't mine, they planted it!" That cast of characters—Yayo, Samantha, El Conejo, Jacobo—they raised up a real shitstorm, and that was when you first really started seeing coke all over the media.

Craziness, Mr. Machi thinks, you'd turn on the TV at two in the afternoon and there was someone talking about how many grams he took a day or where you could get the purest stuff.

"Herminia," he shouts.

"Herminia."

Did that bitch take the maid, too? he wonders. Didn't she even leave a note?

And then he remembers: Mirta usually leaves her notes on the nightstand. He heads up, taking Guillote with him.

But there's no note. No note, no nothing.

He looks through the nightstand—through all the drawers, the cubbyholes and shelves—but he doesn't find anything. Then he sees his wife's closet is open and there are no clothes inside.

Not one stitch.

No note, he thinks, no clothing: it looks like she's taking it seriously this time.

Usually she just packs a few changes of clothes and her big bag of pills when she runs off to live forever at her parents' house in Santa Fe, but emptying out the closet and taking the maid, that's something new.

Alan must have gone with her, Mr. Machi assumes, relieved.

Or—he shakes his head, sighs—to his boyfriend's place.

Suits me, he thinks again, I could do with a bit of rest.

He lifts the telephone from the wall and pushes the 5 on its keypad to speed-dial Eduardo.

"Yes?" his nephew's groggy voice replies.

"Call BMW and get me a new trunk liner and a spare tire."

"Luis?" Eduardo asks, not yet awake. "What? For your car?"

"No, dipshit, for your fucking car: obviously for my car," Mr. Machi responds, overlooking the first two questions.

"But," Eduardo manages to say.

Of course, Mr. Machi has already hung up.

He undresses. He tosses the Adibas tracksuit, the Mike sneakers, and the Reebot polo into a corner.

Later, I'll give that crap to the pool boy, he thinks. Mr. Machi is a bighearted man.

He takes off his underwear, too, but sets it aside: that's name-brand stuff, he's not giving that away.

Naked as he is, he digs through the oak box that houses his collection of cigars and selects one for the occasion. He studies the Cohibas, the Montecristos, the Partagas, finally deciding on an H. Upmann.

Yes, he smiles, pleased with his choice, an H. Upmann Sir Winston, the best Churchill in the world. A cigar to smoke calmly, to take your time with, savoring it on your palate.

After my shower, he decides, and leaves it on the nightstand.

Next to it he cuts out two thick lines of coke from the bag inside the porcelain vase. He looks at the white trails, and for a moment, he hesitates. Then he sucks them up in the blink of an eye.

When I get out of the shower, I'll cut a few more, he thinks, and smiles as his eyes sink deeper into their sockets.

He looks at himself in the mirror on the wall. He admires his naked form. He poses from the front, in profile. Even from the back. Attentively, he looks at his arms, his legs, his chest, his dick, his ass.

I look like a young stallion, he thinks, and expels a cackle.

44

DURING HIS LONG HOUR beneath the steaming hot water, on the other hand, Mr. Machi thinks nothing.

Nothing.

For the first time since all this began, he manages to stop the locomotive barreling ahead in his mind. He doesn't think of complots or coincidences. About what was or what could have been. There's just the abundant jet of water and the steam filling up the room, the hot and humid massage his body receives with gratitude. He finds bumps, bruises, scratches, bites.

But he thinks of nothing.

Nothing.

Not Cesspit, not his wife, not Heredia, not the Reds from the factory.

Nothing.

Not caltrops, not fur handcuffs, not high-priced whores, not even the Glock Alejandro Wilkinson gave him.

Nothing.

It's ages before Mr. Machi decides to get out of the

shower and wrap himself in a towel white and spongy as a spring cloud.

He walks through the house like that, wrapped in the white towel. At the little bar in the living room, he pours himself a shot of Chivas. Then he returns to his bedroom, sniffs a few more lines, and lies down, naked, not yet dry, in bed, on top of the fuzzy green comforter.

Now, yes, he picks up the cigar. He savors the soft but lingering taste, robust, earthy and woody, of the H. Upmann, which he smokes with leisurely patience to keep from burning it down too fast and irritating his nasal passages any further.

I use them too much to damage them, he jokes, and smiles one more time.

Contemplating the cigar, he realizes he's not relaxed all over, no, a certain part of his body is still a little bit restless, starting to wake up, in fact, and he decides to take advantage of Mirta's absence to order a couple of girls from Mariela Báez.

Two, he thinks, or three.

A little group action, that'll do the trick.

And calls.

"Mariela, this is Machi. My wife fucked off somewhere and I'm feeling a little lonely. You wouldn't want to stop by with a few of your best girls," he says.

"But give me three hours," he says, "so I can get a little sleep."

He says: "Let me know when you're close so I can wake up. I'm dead over here."

He hangs up. The word *dead* resounds in the void left inside him by the hot shower, the cigar, and the whiskey. There's a tear in the serenity that's enveloped him since he arrived in El Barrio.

Dead, Mr. Machi thinks.

Dead, he repeats.

But more than a tear, it's a crack. Or better yet, a hairline fracture. Too small for fear, too small even for anxiety. The thing's behind him, and now Mr. Machi asks himself, with aloof curiosity, as if all of it happened to someone else, who the guy could be, the guy someone shot in the face and handcuffed in the trunk of his car. Who could the dude have fucked over so bad for them to finish him off like that, he wonders.

But *who knows* is the only conclusion he comes to.

He puts on a pair of briefs and a cotton T-shirt. Best if he sleeps awhile before the whores show up, he thinks. And that's what he does. And he dreams that all that's happened was nothing more than a farce, a joke, and one by one the figures who embody his fears start filing out from the wings of the stage, until at last the stiff, his face erased by a gunshot and his right hand sawed off, emerges to tell him it's all been a setup, they've pranked him for Trossini's variety show.

Or something like that.

45

HE WAKES UP to the ringing of the phone.

"Luisito, *amor*, we'll be over in fifteen minutes," Mariela Báez says.

Mr. Machi gets out of bed and goes to the bathroom to wash his face and brush his teeth. Once more, in front of the mirror, he inspects his baggy eyes and wrinkles.

"Well, Luis, time to get dressed," he says to the wrinkle-free face with no bags under its eyes, the one he sees reflected in the mirror. He chooses a cologne from his collection—212, Fahrenheit, Terre d'Hermès—and sprays it on his neck, his chest, his wrists and belly.

I'm dressing to the nines tonight! he thinks.

The lavender blue Versace shirt, he thinks.

The Brioni suit I bought last winter in Naples.

Yes, sir.

The Crockett & Jones shoes with the pointed toes.

And one of his red silk ties: maybe the one Thaelman gave him for New Year's, which is one of his favorites.

New money, he thinks, I'll show you new money, you son of a bitch.

In his bedroom, he combs his hair and takes his chosen footwear from the shoe cabinet.

In the safe where he keeps his watches and jewels, he looks for his ruby-encrusted Armani cuff links. Then he goes to the big closet and takes out the lavender blue shirt and the Brioni suit and leaves them on the bed. He looks at the combination with approval and starts to dress. When he's done, he looks himself over in the large mirror.

All that's missing is the tie.

He pauses a moment, Mr. Machi does. Is it worth it to bother with a tie? Mariela and her girls are about to arrive, he thinks, so I won't stay dressed for long.

But he loves his ties. Each and every one in his collection. Almost three hundred of them, all of Italian silk. And so he goes to the closet where he keeps them on their specially designed hangers. He opens the closet and the first thing he sees is the red Marinella Thaelman gave him for New Year's.

Well, the second, actually.

He takes two steps back and falls, Mr. Machi does, feeling a whirlpool opening under his feet, he falls over the nightstand and knocks down the vase called Guillote. There's a crash of porcelain and a dusting of cocaine, but Mr. Machi, at the mercy of his demons, neither sees nor hears.

In the closet, hanging from his favorite silk tie, a stranger—skin sallow, tongue dangling from his mouth as if slowly melting—looks at him with cold eyes.

Cold and dead.

NEWPORT COMMUNITY
LEARNING & LIBRARIES